THE CHILDREN AT THE GATE

EDWARD LEWIS WALLANT

The Children at the Gate

A HARVEST/HBJ BOOK

HARCOURT BRACE JOVANOVICH

NEW YORK AND LONDON

Printed in the United States of America

The lines from "Ash Wednesday," by T. S. Eliot, on page
vii are from *Collected Poems 1909–1962* by T. S. Eliot,
copyright 1936 by Harcourt Brace Jovanovich, Inc.; copyright © 1963, 1964 by T. S. Eliot. Reprinted by permission of
Harcourt Brace Jovanovich, Inc., and Faber and Faber Ltd.

LIBRARY OF CONGRESS CATALOGING IN PUBLICATION DATA

Wallant, Edward Lewis, 1926–1962.
The children at the gate.

(A Harvest/HBJ book)
I. Title.
PZ4.W195Ch   1980   [PS3573.A434]   813'.5'4   79-24169
ISBN 0-15-616861-8

First Harvest/HBJ edition 1980

A B C D E F G H I J

For Joyce

Will the veiled sister pray for
Those who walk in darkness, who chose thee and oppose thee,
Those who are torn on the horn between season and season,
 time and time, between
Hour and hour, word and word, power and power, those who
 wait
In darkness? Will the veiled sister pray
For children at the gate
Who will not go away and cannot pray:
Pray for those who chose and oppose

   O my people, what have I done unto thee.

                              —T. S. Eliot, *Ash Wednesday*

THE CHILDREN AT THE GATE

CHAPTER ONE

DAZED by the daylight, the three of them padded back and forth across the cool floor like penned animals. Even so early in the morning the air was moist and dense, weighted with heat.

Dominic licked his mouth and rolled his eyes. He was suffering from guilt and a hangover, and he groped toward a crucifix to cross himself; he might have been fanning his gross, hairy body with the gesture. Dressed in black, her face pale and sweating, Esther passed her brother almost without noticing him; her near stupor came from a part of her that was in disuse, from the start of some obscure atrophy. Was there enough coffee left in the pot from last night? Probably she would have to add some water, but there ought to be enough for breakfast. *Madonna mia,* save me from this heat, she said to herself, and avoided looking at her daughter: about Theresa, as about the moldering walls of the old house, she could do nothing.

Theresa was sixteen. Her pretty face, with its tan-and-green-flecked eyes, was set slightly awry; more often than not, she kept her lips a little parted. No one in the world knew what was in her head; no one knew if there was anything there at all: she was tuned to a peculiar frequency, and aimlessness was the shape of her life. She moved slowly now over the worn and tedious pattern of the linoleum; she would not stop until somebody stopped her.

Only her brother, Angelo DeMarco, had come awake like a light going on, and known as much as he could know, right from the first moment of consciousness. Fully dressed and clean, he moved among the others with an air of purpose; his lean face was scornful, his fierce gaze picked things to pieces. He looked into the bathroom mirror to see if he had done what he could for his appearance. His straight black Indian hair was combed neatly; his almost lipless face, which made him look much older than nineteen, was shaved impeccably and shone with cleanliness. One eye was tan, the other almost black, and they stared back at him with cool amusement. His nose, broken three times in fights, was flat and bent; his smile showed a broken tooth. There wasn't one feature that hadn't been insulted many times, either directly or by implication, and he was proud of that fact; it made his face dear to him.

"God damn you, Angelo!" his uncle shouted from the dining room. "How many times I got to tell you not to hang your goddam tie on the cross? How 'bout you have some respect, hah?"

"Forgive me, Father, for I have sinned," Angelo intoned.

"Angelo!" Dominic came to the door of the bathroom and raised a hand. Angelo grinned, and Dominic, who punished only from a distance now, growled impotently before going back to the dining room for his shoes. When Angelo was younger, Dominic had sometimes beaten him, never badly and always with sufficient provocation. The boy had seemed to invite punishment, but his uncle had never been cruel; the beatings *had* hurt him more than they hurt Angelo. And one day Dominic had looked into the boy's contemptuous eyes and had seen that, despite his own great advantage in weight and strength, he was outmatched. What had begun in him as an expectancy of love had turned into bewildered crankiness, and he was unhappy in his own house all the time.

Angelo entered the bedroom and stopped in front of the dresser, where some two dozen books stood in an uneven rank. Among them was *A Child's Book of Natural Science,* a thin, gray, austere volume, with a text as forbidding as its binding, printed in a thick black outmoded type and filled with dry line drawings like those in a dictionary. It should never have appealed to a child and perhaps its original owner had never read it; it was the kind of thing one picks up at an auction, a bargain for a quarter. Because it had been his father's, Angelo had at one time been filled with a passion for the book, which had been thrust into his hands on a day of death when he reeled among a crowd of strangers. It had unlocked a landscape for him, and he left it now in honorable pasture, a child's book, but father to all the rest—to the books of astronomy, zoology, physics, and chemistry, and the scrapbook with clippings on scientific subjects from magazines and newspapers. A great deal of what he read he had trouble understanding, but he persistently reread, having some confidence in repetition. Now he selected a thick volume with a bookmark in it and headed for the kitchen. He looked like a worker priest, divorced from the incense and the trappings yet somehow imbued with a priest's fierce dedication.

He gazed blankly at the panoply of religious objects that cluttered the house. There were pictures of saints and Madonnas, some of them small reproductions of Renaissance paintings, others like sentimental bubble-gum cards. There were a half-dozen versions of the Crucifixion, plaster statues of Jesus and Mary, dusty crosses in wood and brass and nickel. And there was a ceramic cast of a saint's severed hand, which reached for the comfort of a bleeding heart embroidered on a satin cushion.

Angelo knew that his mother bought such artifacts whenever she worried about her deep, dim sensations of sin, and he sometimes considered throwing all of them into a rubbish can, not in malice or anger, but simply in his passion for neatness.

"Angelo," his mother cried in a minor key as he stepped into the kitchen. "Why do you get him all upset like that? How many times I got to tell you? Do I need him all upset?" She rushed at him in her dusty black, and for a moment seemed about to throw herself on him. But all of this was familiar to Angelo, and he stopped and she stopped.

"Don' antagonize, *please?*" she said.

"Sure, sure," he said mildly, looking past her.

And although she stood close to him, she had not looked at him directly. Her face had been squeezed of passion and there remained only a confused petulance. Her mouth was dry and scored by many tiny vertical cracks; her skin was waxy. Once Angelo had amused himself with the idea that he and Theresa were the products of artificial insemination, so unlikely did it seem that his mother had lain with a living man. In trying to analyze his feelings for her he had sometimes recalled her demonstrations of affection—those hazy times when he had been sick and she had placed her cool hand on his head, or the rare occasions when she had called his name, dreamily, gently, and for no discernible reason. But such moments had been too scattered to have stimulated any cumulative response in him. Mostly, he and his mother spoke around each other and avoided meeting each other's eyes.

Dominic came in and sat down at the table, grumbling, savoring the dregs of his irritation, and glared at the reheated coffee. "I can't even eat," he complained. "He made my stomach get all crapped up. He hung his tie on the *cross*."

"Angelo," Esther bleated.

"Just gimme the coffee, forget the rest," Dominic said. Then, as he gazed gloomily at the light in the yard, his expression weakened; his mouth went slack; dismay came feebly into his dark, still-handsome eyes. "Cheez, *fa caldo,* must be eighty already."

"Paper says maybe ninety today. And I got to go to the Sodality tonight." Esther sighed to convince her brother that it was duty rather than pleasure. "I'll leave your supper."

"Okay, okay." Dominic reached for a doughnut as though he were doing her a favor.

Esther stood leaning against the stove and sipped her coffee. Outside, the voices of the neighborhood were close and loud. In the crowded houses people woke to violence and spoke in roars, asserting themselves before the specter of a treadmill day. Even the occasional bursts of laughter sounded heated and angry. The air was full of bird twitter, but the noise of the people overwhelmed it.

Angelo ate his toast delicately, staring across the table at Theresa.

"Eat your breakfast," he murmured. He had a special tone of voice that could always reach her, and Esther told people,

7

"Angelo can handle her." She would scold her daughter through her son; even Dominic, on those rare occasions when he attempted to communicate with Theresa, would do so through Angelo. But they were never quite relaxed when he spoke to her on his own; they sensed something unwholesome in the relationship.

"Come on, Theresa, your coffee will get cold. You know you don't like it cold. That's right, yeah—and your bread too." He leaned slightly toward her, his dark, mean face imperceptibly milder, his voice soft and monotonous, yet seeming to have the power to carry a great distance.

As children they had been together constantly; he had been welded to her by his loneliness and by the hostility to other children that he himself perpetuated. In the quiet, almost dreamlike little games he had created with only half his attention, he had spoken to her steadily. It was as though he had used her for an echoing surface; with her he said aloud all the things he could never say to anyone else, things that needed saying to prevent his taciturnity from drying the living moisture of what he was. Sometimes neighborhood boys had called humorous insults at Theresa, without particularly vicious intent, and Angelo had hurled his skinny, steely body at them, tearing and punching with a fury out of all proportion to their innocent cruelty. The boys had run off, frightened not so much by Angelo's attack as by the expression on his face, calm and determined and clearly intent on total destruction; they could *feel* that he would kill them if he could. After they were gone he returned to Theresa with that same terrifying calm. She had learned his voice as she had learned breathing; she didn't know enough to love.

Dominic belched and lit a cigarette. The smoke was lively in the shabby cave of the room; out in the next yard, visible through the window, an old man tended his tomato plants

8

like children, with impatient tenderness; there was a smell of grapes and garbage and hot greenery. Dominic pondered his state of grace and wondered if he would be able to remember everything for Confession. Sourly, he considered carrying around a little pad and pencil, noting his sins as they occurred. Then, remembering the sweaty struggle with a woman last night, he winced and relinquished the frayed scrap of humor. And how would he tell the priest about his crimes in his own house, how justify his constant irritation and his dislike of his nephew and his niece? Well, for one thing, he could never forgive Angelo for not being burdened with Confession himself. Why wasn't that kid afraid of God like normal people? And the girl! She disgusted him and he couldn't help showing it. If only she *looked* like an idiot, one of those kids with Chinese eyes. It got him on edge sometimes, seeing her pretty face that looked almost normal; he kept expecting her to speak sensibly. No, the truth was that the two of them—and even his sister, who lived and acted like a nun—had over the years turned him into an irritable, nervous man. They made him drink more than he would have; they made him explode and then suffer guilt for it. One of these days . . .

Esther sighed. "It's going to be so hot. I don't know . . ."

Theresa followed Angelo with her eyes as he got up from the table without a word and left the kitchen. Carrying the biology book under his arm, he went through the dining room to the front door, stopped briefly for an obscene gesture at the collection of religious paraphernalia, and sauntered out of the house.

The street was always in a state of sleazy undress, but Angelo, who had lived here most of his life, walked indifferently over a scattering of pink and red confetti. Crepe-paper bunting was strewn along fences, and colored bulbs dangled from wires above the street: they were always celebrating, holy this and holy that. One front yard had a cement peacock encrusted with pieces of mirror; another had a shrewish Virgin standing in a zinc tub, where a few disconsolate lily pads floated among cigarette butts and popsicle papers. From the doorway of a tiny grocery a bald man in an apron peered out suspiciously. In one of his windows stood a quarter wheel of cheese, a few loaves of Italian bread, and three lemons; the other window had a sun-faded cigarette poster that showed a man and a woman on a beach that seemed choked with smog. A smell of cheese and salami came from the doorway.

Angelo walked with his hands in his pockets, the book squeezed between his arm and his body. With his wide, skinny shoulders and short neck, he seemed to be hunched up against a nagging cold despite the hot July morning. Now and then someone grunted a greeting to him, and he responded with the faint lip movement a prisoner uses. Girls he had gone to school with, dressed in cheap, tight dresses that emphasized their breasts and buttocks, nodded carefully to him, sometimes muttering his name coolly, unwilling to encourage his friendliness, yet somehow apprehensive about offending him. His response to them was merely an exasperated lidding of his eyes.

Some of the younger men who, a few years earlier, had been his tormentors went by him as though he were invisible. He was a familiarly aggravating sight, and he oppressed them because they remembered what an unreasonable victim he had been. One husky youth stood in his gateway lighting a cigarette, his eyes flickering briefly over Angelo. Once he had twisted Angelo's arm for mild amusement but had encountered horror instead. The scuffle had become a grim, odd slaughter. Despite the fact that he punched Angelo to the ground over and over again, he wondered who was slaughtering who. It went on for a long time, the smaller boy's face coating with blood and dust and the big boy growing more frightened each time Angelo got up and came at him. It began to seem that he would have to kill Angelo or be killed by him. Over and over, with nightmarish patience, the small, skinny boy attacked, clawing, gouging, kicking. When others had finally stopped the strange fight, the big boy wanted to cry with relief. After that they had passed each other by without a sign of recognition.

In one form or another the same thing had happened repeatedly. Sometimes the encounters hadn't been physical; occasionally there had been assaults of pitying kindness. Angelo knew how to deal with those as well. People left him alone now and he existed in a satisfying solitude. Nor was he dulled by his solitary state; a constant, merciless curiosity animated him, and often he was stimulated to a sort of cold joy when some new fact was revealed to him. He knew he was fortunate in having the intelligence to see his situation for what it was. He read avidly, at any hour, in any place, muttering triumphant oaths when a sentence or a word opened up a myth to the reality of bone and blood cell. When others had murmured piously that his father had gone to heaven, he had punctured the image by learning about the electric impulses of the brain and the nature of organic decomposition. They had whined about love and the need to learn his Catechism, and he had accepted beatings from Dominic and threats from the priests, strong in his dissection of their motives. At school he had seen so clearly the green scale that tainted the Golden Rule, which was hypocrisy and cruelty. By contrast, his own ruthlessness struck him as wholesome. He had endured their assaults and come out strong and fresh, and full of a melancholy gaiety. And even if he was occasionally visited by mystifying pain, a rare dusting of odd sorrow, he accepted that too. It kept him on his toes and prevented dullness and complacency. All he wanted was *to know*. The one thing that could incite him to true human anger was delusion.

He crossed a railroad bridge as a sleek diesel shot under; wires and tracks were threads of hot silver. Passing men in work clothes, he seemed a sort of poseur in his shabby white shirt, his threadbare tie, his shoes that were round-heeled and leprous with age. There was a bizarre contrast between his assassin face and the decorum of the tie and the shirt and the neatly parted black hair; there was an oddness in his walk, which was effortless and upright, his head so still he could have balanced a jug of water on it.

He was poor and shabby, but he looked down on everyone because he knew he was his own man, and the yearnings that sometimes nagged him were small payment for the freedom he felt. Mostly he was unassailable within the cool vessel he had made of himself, able to patch the minor cracks of lonely moments, to deflect the encroachment of a girl's laughter or of people's murmured conversations on porches or doorsteps in the summer night.

Now he was passing the old churches on the green, and the university where tall, well-fed students wore old clothes with insouciant grace. A man with black hair impinged momentarily on his consciousness and he wondered about the color of his father's hair, but this sort of thing had happened before, and did not disturb him: as he learned what he could, he put his father together from the parts of himself that he understood.

Pigeons settled like a quilt, with a swoosh of air. The pavement felt hot beneath his thin soles. A faint ringing testified to the heat, and he smelled tar. Over all the buildings, over the spaces of bare earth, over the work-bound people and the cars and buses, the dense heat hung like an immense bell jar that threatened in tiny ticking sounds to crack, so that everything would be destroyed in the naked burn of the sun.

Angelo reached his cousin's store. It was set back from the street behind a small plaza in which there were four rectangles of earth, each surrounded by a low, thorny hedge; they were barren except for the one directly in front of the store, and that only sprouted the steel poles that supported the sign.

DeMarco Pharmacy.

Inside, he breathed the familiar odors of talc and malt and the composite of all the herbs and liquids Frank used in the prescription room. The woodwork was stained mahogany; the floor was worn to splinters, which caught unpleasantly on the broom when he swept up in the evening. The store was overloaded with stock and there was a constant creaking, as though at any moment the whole place might collapse under its weight. Frank sold everything from liquor to bathroom scales; Angelo knew how it frustrated his cousin to have to admit he was out of stock on something, and the cellar was a warren of esoteric merchandise that he might someday be asked for.

Angelo slipped his book into the cabinet where the cigarettes were stored and went back to the prescription room, where Frank was busy making his own brand of cough medicine. He had a large bottle of simple syrup tilted up over a funnel and he grinned at Angelo as he poured.

"*Come sta, paesan'?*" he said.

"One of these days you're gonna get in trouble with the Pure Food and Drug."

"Not unless my own cousin turns fink." Frank gazed placidly at the bottle, seeming to take great pleasure in the steady transfer of liquid.

"Don't your conscience bother you?"

"What, conscience!" Frank yelled. "It's just as good as Parke-Davis. I put in a smidgin of codeine, just a kiss of terpin hydrate, some nice pure syrup, and—*voylah*—cough medicine! Nah . . ." He shook his head with tolerant scorn. "Ethics is flexible, my friend, I got my own personal code. Besides . . ." He carefully lifted the funnel and placed it in the neck of another of the row of bottles. "I operate on the psychosomatic theory. Medicine helps people if they think it helps them. Just look at my stuff compared to the other brands. Same color, same taste. The label is very dignified— I had Manuccivello from the printer shop design it, cost me five bucks. Look at the brand name, DeMay Pharmaceutical —if that don't have practically a *smell* of integrity I don't know what does. On top of everything, it's a bargain. Chrissake, I sell it twenty cents cheaper than the others."

"You're a crook, Frank," Angelo said, relaxing in his cousin's sunny fraudulence.

"Just words. You're a crook if you're stupid and vulgar. Me, I'm a business man." Suddenly he began to laugh. He was short and square, with sly, humorous eyes and wide-spaced teeth that gave him a cannibalistic look. "Trouble with you, *compa'*, you're only a amateur cynic. You're too fierce. With you it's either black or white. You're not flexible. You discovered a few little lies, so you won't accept nothing at face value. My secret is I'm graceful and relaxed. I mean, there's crooks and crooks, there's nonsense and there's things you can't never expect to make sense."

"You're a real sage, Frank, but you don't have a straight bone in your body. Don't try and snow *me* with your double talk."

Frank looked briefly toward heaven before he moved on to the next bottle. He liked Angelo and respected his sardonic intelligence. Besides, he had been friendly with his father and felt a comfortable obligation to the son. Not that this prevented him from working Angelo some eighty hours a week and grossly underpaying him. Frank was crass and stingy because under the thinnest veneer of education he was a poor Wooster Street boy, too, and like many peasants who acquire some money, he was jealous and fearful about it. He might feel pain if he ever had to sacrifice Angelo for money, but he would probably do so. Yet Angelo found his situation bearable because of the intangible fringe benefits of his cousin's personality. His job certainly could be described as a rut, but to Angelo so were all other jobs, and he was less concerned with where it led than with the width of it. He never had to contend with humiliation there.

A fly buzzed against the screened back door; the stock freighted the shelves audibly; the liquid went *glunk, glunk, glunk* into the bottles. Angelo gazed at his cousin's muddy, bemused eyes that watched his wealth accumulate. A Saint Christopher medal was a darkish shape under his thin batiste shirt; a thread of sweat ran down his neck. Angelo considered the happiness of the smug and wondered if he ever envied it.

"Why don't you fill the syrup pumps, Ange, while you're resting?"

"While I'm resting," Angelo echoed.

He went to the front of the store and poured the syrups, which emitted a fruity, confectionery scent. Then he wiped up the sticky spillings and moved to the cupboard to replenish the cigarette bins. But, kneeling there, he was halted by his book. He opened it and, as was his habit, fell into the reading like the victim of a spell. Squatting, a carton of cigarettes in one hand, the book opened in the other, he frowned and moved his lips slightly to reinforce what he read.

If now the genes for color and the genes for length are arranged in pairs, we have CCS. It is thus seen that such an animal is homozygous with respect to hair color. . . .

15

" 'Homozygous,' " he muttered, looking blankly into the cupboard.

A customer rapped a coin impatiently on the marble counter.

"Angelo," Frank wailed from the back room. "Wake up, will you?"

Angelo tore off a piece of the carton to mark his place. Standing, he stared flatly at the jaundiced face and linty hair. Was this old man homozygous?

"Gimme a lemon Coke," the old man said. "Not too sweet."

"Yes *sir*." Angelo briskly squirted syrup into a glass, added seltzer, and clocked the glass onto the counter. "Fifteen cents."

"I wanted a *small* lemon Coke."

Angelo shrugged innocently. You always gave them the large when they didn't specify. Frank's true apprentice rang up the sale, and the ding of the cash register signaled the beginning of the workday.

The morning went quickly. Nurses, doctors, and orderlies from the hospital came in singly or in humming twos and threes. Most of the customers knew Angelo and, knowing him, only nodded or gave the briefest word of greeting. The personality attraction was Frank, and they accepted the taciturn youth as though he were not worth distaste.

Terse, quick-moving, and dextrous, as dark as the woodwork, he made sodas and sandwiches, sold sundries and cosmetics and patent medicines, knowing where everything was. Perhaps the old habitués might even feel a slight nostalgia for him if he should ever leave, just as they might if the store were redecorated or the old overhead fan replaced by air conditioning. Oddly formal in his buttoned-up shirt and tie, while the boss worked casually in an open-necked sportshirt, he seemed to have a solidity that Frank vaguely appreciated. He was a one-man staff, peculiarly professional in a job that required little skill. Sometimes Frank himself had to turn to him with a questioning expression when a rare request puzzled him. Angelo remembered where a dusty truss lay cobwebbed in the cellar, knew which of the multitude of tiny drawers held prophylactics, combs, pessaries, garter belts, elastic stockings, douche bags, ballpoint pens. He knew prices, fixed and flexible, and in an emergency could even fill certain capsules. In short, he was superior to Frank in almost all the workings of the store except for a rapport with the customers. Angelo was polite and prompt, but he gave nothing that wasn't paid for directly.

Frank acted as the shepherd, driving the customers to Angelo with jokes and double talk, his face livening more and more with each ring of the cash register. From time to time he slipped his finger between the buttons of his shirt to touch the Saint Christopher medal. He considered his sins compensated for by his good will. He slapped backs, pinched buttocks, asked intimate questions with his arm around shoulders, his canine face intensely interested and sympathetic.

The morning and the noon hour went by in a rattle of glasses, a babble of voices, a clink of money.

Then it was two o'clock. Angelo had finished his sandwich in the back room and had reluctantly returned his book to the cigarette cupboard. For a few minutes he stared at the baroque reds and golds of the cigar-box labels, musing in the sudden quiet. The overhead fan moved slowly beneath the dirty ceiling; it made a creak that reminded him of a huge wheel he had once seen in a movie, a wheel that white and piebald cattle rotated without end. In the mild daze of heat and silence, staring microscopically at the heraldic letters (*Panetelas*—what a funny word!), he could hear the dust shift in the slow movement of air.

Suddenly Frank whistled warningly. Angelo turned.

Frank made the hitchhiker sign with his thumb. "Get going, *compa'*," he said. Angelo looked at him with a blank expression. "Wake up, wake up, the hospital. It's almost two thirty."

But in the way Angelo moved, it could be seen that the expression had not been one of surprise. He took a long strip of cash-register paper and a stub of pencil. His stomach tightened slightly, and his lean face assumed the grimly patient quality it had worn during all his long, painful fights with bigger boys.

A slow, protracted hiss was F-shaped as he exhaled with his upper teeth pressed hard into his lip.

The Sacred Heart Hospital. Talk about Calvary.

CHAPTER TWO

HE passed the main entrance, whose granite cross was spattered with bird droppings, moved along the big stretch of lawn upon which a sheep munched steadily, then went down the ambulance ramp and into the emergency entrance, where the hospital policeman nodded at him. The familiar ether odor struck him, and he ignored the sweet disapproval of the plaster Madonna as he pressed the elevator button. His territory.

On the first floor the elevator picked up Lebedov, a lion-faced old orderly with a powerful, broken-looking body. Lebedov, who wheeled in a cart of bedpans and bottles, never spoke to anyone; addressed directly, he muttered or grunted.

Now he put his great, stiff hands on the rubber-covered bar of the cart and stared dully at Angelo's tie. On the second floor, a stretcher bearing a dark child was wheeled on by another orderly, an effeminate man named Howard Miller. Two student nurses followed, whispering about some reputed Adonis among the internes. In their white caps and jumpers, their true-blue blouses, they seemed starched to an unreal crispness. Howard Miller winked at Angelo, his face performing its usual nervous gyrations. Angelo ignored him. Jammed into a corner by the stretcher and Lebedov's cart, he looked at the dark cables through the grating near the ceiling of the elevator.

"He's at *least* six feet tall," one student nurse said.

"I *love* his hair," the other one answered.

The child on the stretcher stared at the ceiling of the elevator as if she wished to remember it. Lebedov's hands moved in a slow pulse on the bar of the cart, and the elevator moved as slowly upward. The child's throat was bandaged. The young nurses giggled.

On the third floor Lebedov took his cart off and an ivory-faced nun replaced him.

"Sister Louise," Angelo murmured at her stiff nod, his tone indicating he was only identifying an object for himself. The two student nurses stopped whispering and exchanged sour looks behind the nun's back. The quiet whirring of the elevator became softer and softer as they rose farther from the motor in the basement.

At the fifth and top floor, the nurses helped Howard Miller wheel the stretcher away; the little girl lay staring upward, watching the ceilings change. Sister Louise got off and Angelo followed. At the head of the corridor, in a blue-plaster robe, Jesus held His hands out as though for alms. From the chapel nearby came the monotonous, slightly hoarse voice of another nun: "Hail Mary, full of grace, the Lord is with thee: blessed art thou among women. . . ."

Angelo nodded to the greetings of nurses and nuns, his eyes seeing only their reflections in the gleaming brown linoleum, his strip of cash-register paper hanging from his fingers.

"Hi, Angelo," Nurse Sullivan said.

"Hi," he answered, looking at her pretty face. Her smile made some sensation in him, and he quickly explained to himself the natural workings of desire. She had a full, curved body, which was stylized by the stiff white uniform; her legs were voluptuous in the white stockings, her prominent calves set unusually low.

"Grouchy," she said, stopping in his path. "Why don't you smile once in a while?" Her voice was lilting and jovial, her complexion very white, blotched here and there by soft pink patches; it was the kind of skin that showed marks at the slightest touch. Pure and simple, he said to himself, I want to screw her. The fact that this was impossible caused him a slight pang; he had the idea that never in his life would he possess a woman on terms that would be acceptable to him.

"I have an ugly smile, it scares people."

"Don't you know that it takes more muscles to frown than it does . . ."

"To smile," he supplied in duet with her. "What's the big deal with smiling?" She was really stupid, but he bent his mouth for her.

"I like cheerful people." She showed her own smile in demonstration; her small white teeth were set in overlarge gums like those of some Filipino women. "I hate sourpusses."

"Well, that lets me out. I guess we'll just have to break it off."

She laughed delightedly; the sound was incongruous and almost improper in the dim, gleaming corridor. For years

21

they had been carrying on the same banter, and at one time she had almost tempted Angelo to the insanity of daydream. Now, however, she was just a symbol in his occasional erotic blazings.

"Anyhow," she said, touching the back of her hair. "I'm too old for you, Angelo dear. When you're sixty, I'll be seventy."

"We could worry about that when we come to it," he said, running his eyes down her figure and making a clicking sound with his mouth. He was so removed from eligibility that even lewd gestures were taken as jokes.

"Oh *Angelo!*" She gave his cheek a pat and walked on past him, smelling of perfume. The swish of her clothing sent a minor chill through him, but he shrugged in the manner of his street and went about his business.

He began at the room near the solarium.

"DeMarco's Pharmacy, want anything?"

A yellow-faced old man, who had a tube in his nose, shook his head.

"DeMarco's, get you something?"

A middle-aged Jew stared absently from his oxygen tent to the crucifix on his wall. It seemed to take almost a half minute for Angelo's voice to reach him, and he turned slowly toward the door. The oxygen compressor whined and clinked like an old refrigerator.

"Well, how about it? Do you want to order something from the store?" Angelo breathed, used to reiteration, neither bored nor willing, but faithful. "The drugstore," he said. Finally the man shook his head, negatively and very slowly.

In and out of the rooms, Angelo solicited men and women, girls big-eyed with pain, old people peering dimly from the stink of their bodies. "DeMarco's Pharmacy. Need any talcum, scented alcohol, stationery, ice cream . . . ?" His questions probed the pain-ridden or those expectant of pain, those who were giving birth and those who were giving up. And he knew that his very heedlessness was what made him bearable to them. Beside beds, from doorways, he spoke and was answered, and he took down the orders mechanically. His already corrupted sense of smell deteriorated further among the odors of ether and feces and sweat. And if he was brutalized by their constant assault, and if no pity was elicited in him, it was partly because he was in and out of there so often that the births and extinctions had no history. Besides, he knew the structure of the human body from his study; he held the vascular, skeletal, muscular drawings against his brain like a talisman against pain.

"Ice cream, magazines, cosmetics, cigarettes, sandwiches," he called into the wards and the semiprivate rooms. Gradually the list grew and he reached a point where he had to write smaller and smaller. Each time he left the store he seemed to take a longer strip of paper, and each time it turned out too short.

His last call was in the children's pavilion across the cement yard from the main building. In that ward the nuns in their long white robes glided back and forth as though they had no feet, and Jesus was a rosy plaster infant in His mother's arms. The afternoon sun slanted through the windows onto the dust in the air, glowed weakly on brown-painted beds, and threw cagelike shadows on the linoleum floors. The children looked dim and old, their heads up against the walls in shadow.

But some of them had spending money, and he solicited them without condescension.

"I want a chocolate ice-cream soda with coffee ice cream," said a blonde girl who was blindered by bandages and new to the handicap, so that she spoke in a completely wrong direction and turned, startled and guilty, only when Angelo confirmed her order from up close.

A boy in a plaster cast from his chest down said he wanted a malted milk and a package of Oreo cookies. The delicacy of his face was shattered by heavy, thirsty-looking lips. Angelo took his order and moved on.

"Good afternoon, Angelo," a nun said to him.

"Afternoon, Sister Cecilia," he answered tonelessly.

"Angelo," said another nun.

"Sister Mary Frances," he replied.

He recognized the small, dark girl he had seen in the elevator less than an hour before and stopped at her bed. "Want something from the store?" he asked.

She began to write something on the pad beside her bed, her silky black hair shielding most of her face from him. When she was done, she handed him the note. In first grade lettering, it read: "ONE CUP VINILA ICE CREM." She peered at him to see if he understood her desire, and when he looked back at her and nodded, he noticed that her bandaged neck held a small perforated disk in the gauze.

"Large?" He held his hands wide apart. "Or small?" he closed the gap between his hands.

She just turned her head awkwardly to the night table, where a dime lay next to a small stuffed panda and a Negro doll.

"Okay," he said, squeezing her order in at the bottom of the page.

The card at the end of her bed said that her name was Maria Alvarez and that her most recent temperature was 100.5. But she caught his study of the chart and with her immense, prune-colored eyes defied him to know her by that brief description.

24

"That's the small cup," he said to her. She stared back, making no move toward her pad.

He looked around the ward to see if he might have missed someone. A small phonograph was playing "The Farmer in the Dell." The children's limbs under the sheets were like a range of low, snow-covered mountains; their faces were dark and quietly alive. The nuns moved busily among them, and Angelo knew why they concentrated their energies there; the youthful patients were more impressionable and would ultimately confuse the professional comfort of the ministering hands with the dead benevolence of the plaster image, thus to carry the lie forever, or anyhow for as long as it would matter. For the first time that day, the legend depressed him, and he moved out of the ward aware of a faint irritation.

In the cement yard between the buildings, he stopped to look at the new hospital under construction on the neighboring block. It would replace the old Sacred Heart buildings. Squinting in the brilliant afternoon, he followed its height as it rose into the blue summer sky, gleaming white, simple, monolithic. It was set in a vast open area where there would be no darkness cast upon it, no shadows except those it cast itself. A din of pneumatic drills came from it, and dust hovered over the lower floors, so that the tall, slender building seemed like a rocket on the brink of launching. He compared it to the crouching pile of the old hospital, with its soot-gathering cement work under the green copper roof, its vent holes and overhangs, which the pigeons took advantage of. The new hospital soared and was heedlessly open to light; it could have been alabaster. But how different would it be inside? They would take all the dust collectors from the old building, all the statues and bas-reliefs. And the people.

He shrugged and headed back to the store to fill the orders.

CHAPTER THREE

Esther's voice rose from a clatter of crockery. "Angelo! Tell her to wash her face, hah? And comb her hair for her. She's funny today, won't let me near her." The dishes clattered again, with submerged violence, as she hurried to get ready for Sodality.

Dominic walked through the house puffing on a black cigar. He was a long way from morning now; he was a long way from irritation, too, and could look contemplatively at things that earlier had rubbed him raw. He was even capable of sadness. He stood in the doorway watching Angelo comb Theresa's hair and reminisced, touched by the irony of the scene. The long oval mirror in front of which Theresa sat was an heirloom his mother had brought from Abruzzi long ago, to reflect the beauty of succeeding generations, and now it reflected the dim, faintly warped face of his niece. Ah, well, he thought, children of God, poor bastards. Even that little rat Angelo must be miserable inside. Why is he such an outlaw? Eh, that was life, they were born like that; her, *tutta pazza;* him, ugly and mean. What are you gonna do?

Angelo held his sister's narrow head with one hand; the skull was like a downy egg, fragile and strange; the hair was long and shiny, fine-textured, the color of maple syrup in a bottle with the light shining through it. He felt a curiously painful pleasure in the way the teeth of the comb bit into the hair and raked it into gleaming strands.

Theresa stared into the mirror at his reflection, her expressionless eyes blinking slowly. To get at another part of her head, Angelo shifted his hand, and for a moment it rested on her soft, damp cheek. Instinctively she tilted her head and trapped the hand between cheek and shoulder, her eyes closed. Angelo's face darkened and he jerked away from her with a dart of guilt and pain.

"Come on, Theresa," he said harshly, but in his voice for her. She stayed, however, with her head tilted onto her shoulder, her eyes closed yet seeming to flicker behind the translucent lids. Why did she get under his skin sometimes, he wondered? Why did her silence, her brainless little motions, somehow undermine him?

"Theresa," he said, holding the comb up to the mirror in entreaty.

But she sat with her head fallen onto her shoulder, her eyes closed, and it was as though something had risen in her, something with a shape and a dimension she could not handle, something whose size and hardness might have broken whatever was breakable in her. And Angelo, quick to sound

27

and light, alert to all possibilities, was caught by her kinetic idiocy and stood for a while as still as she. If he was not moved, he was at least impressed by what she arrested in him.

They stayed in the muted light of dusk like creatures imbedded in amber, so that Dominic saw them with a strange distaste and unease; until finally the sight of them became insufferable and he turned away, suddenly anxious for the smell of the street.

When he got back to the store, Angelo felt unusually tired, and the prospect of his evening trip to the hospital was particularly oppressive. He tore off a much longer strip of cash-register paper, knew immediately that it would not be long enough, and was out of the store, so quickly that Frank was still talking to him from the back room after he was gone.

They were saying Complin in the fifth-floor chapel; the lethargic voices scraped at the evening air and made him restless. Sullivan passed, on her way home, her winged cap in her hand; she blew him a kiss, and he shrugged wearily at her. The halls were quiet and almost empty; behind closed doors patients were being sponged and made comfortable for the night. Lebedov wheeled his perpetual cart of bedpans and urinal bottles, his face mottled and grim.

Angelo began his tour.

"Anything from DeMarco's? Ice cream, magazines, toothpaste, toilet water, lipsticks, eau de cologne . . ."

In one room a husky young man with thin, brick-colored hair lay tossing his head back and forth in sleep, grinding his teeth and murmuring incomprehensibly. In another a priest was giving Extreme Unction behind a half-closed door; outside the door some of the family stood crying quietly. For a moment Angelo was tempted to offer consolation in the form of ice cream or scented alcohol; he refrained only be-

28

cause the act would be misconstrued as cruel. He smiled slightly, moved on, and finished taking his orders.

When he came back from the pharmacy with what seemed the heaviest carton he had ever carried, he went first to the children's pavilion. Standing in the dim light near the door, he squinted at his cramped handwriting and tried to place each child's face by the item ordered. When he thought he had it figured out, he picked up the carton and started down the row of beds. Here and there a child whimpered; one girl, her voice almost all whisper, called for her mother. Somehow the darkness seemed to exaggerate their pain, and the room was phantasmagoric in the dimness of the night lights. The movement of a small limb or the flap of a blind or the rustle of a nun's garments set the gloom eddying in widening ripples.

In that enlargement of the minuscule, an orderly Angelo had never seen before moved out from between two beds, turned, and smiled, his face long and pearly in the dimness. Startled by the tall, narrow white shape, Angelo realized he was gaping at the man. He looked down at his carton and said, "What, are you new here?"

"That's right, *bubi*, brand new. I'm Sammy, and, believe *me*, it never rains but it pours."

Angelo just stood there, gazing stupidly at what he could see of the white, foolish-looking face.

"Do you know where you're going?" the orderly asked in a high, soft voice. "Come on, I got a flashlight, I'll light you." So the luminous oval went gliding along the floor ahead of Angelo, from one bed to the next.

Angelo handed a chilled carton to the boy with the delicate face, and counted out the change in the light held by the orderly. Suddenly the beam swept upward and revealed the thick mouth sucking avidly at the straws.

"Ahh, that was what he wanted," the orderly said in an expiring voice. "What flavor is it, kid?"

"Strawberry." The boy went on sucking.

"Oh, I like strawberry good enough," the orderly said. "But not as much as chocolate. It's all right when it's fresh-fruit flavor, but I don't like the artificial. Which is that?"

The boy held the carton away and studied it doubtfully. "I don't know." He shrugged. "Anyway, it's good."

"Come on," Angelo said brusquely, "if you're so generous with that light. I got ice cream melting here."

The beam skittered over the bedding to the floor and led him out to the aisle. He moved toward the statue at the far end, and the light skipped ahead of him, stopping when he did, beginning to learn his reflexes.

He put an ice-cream cup into the hand of the blonde girl, and the light fixed on her bandaged eyes. Framed in the darkness, the gauze had a disquieting texture; where it met the smooth, fair skin of her cheek, it looked monstrous.

"Some help," Angelo grumbled as he groped for the spoon he had dropped. But the light held on her bandages until its brightness seemed to ignite them.

"What's the matter with your eyes?" the orderly asked. "Are you blind?"

Angelo hissed involuntarily.

"I don't know." The girl spoke in a matter-of-fact voice. "Anyhow, I wouldn't be able to see with this darn thing on. I used to be able to see. . . . Oh, how should I know?"

"Sometimes I close my eyes to imagine I'm like blind," the orderly said. "It's hard, though, because I know I can always open them. I bet you hate not being able to open your eyes."

"The bandages itch."

"What is it, just ice cream, or a sundae?"

"Maple-nut sundae."

"Can I have a taste?"

"Uh-*uh*," she said, emphatically shaking her head.

"Look, if you're *gonna* hold that light for me . . . I don't have all night," Angelo said.

They reached Maria Alvarez, and he put a carton of soda on her table with a wet rattle of ice chunks. "You're a penny short," he said indifferently as he swept the coins from the table top into his hand. But she ignored him, aiming her eyes at the figure behind the light.

"*Ssssss, ffffff—sssss, ffffff*," went the orderly.

She gazed at the dazzle from which the sound came, and then, squinting, wrote on the pad: "WAT ARE YOU MAKEING THAT SOND FOR?"

"I'm imitating that thing in your throat."

She looked disdainful; she, after all, had the actual thing. But she continued to search for his face in the dark, even after they had moved on.

The beam led Angelo to the doorway, where it faded somewhat in the glow of the night light. He looked back at the ward, wondering if he had served everyone, spun around, and carried his carton through the doorway the orderly was holding open for him.

They walked together across the yard without speaking. Angelo stubbornly kept his eyes away from the egg of light on the concrete, but the white uniform beside him was a nagging blur. Their footsteps echoed from the stone of the buildings, and the sky seemed low enough to trap the sound. Suddenly the white figure broke away and loped ahead. Angelo could just make it out against the building before a rectangle of light appeared; the orderly held the door open and bowed him in.

"I'm not used to such service," Angelo said.

"Stick with me, *boychik*—you'll have diamonds as big as

lumps of coal." When the elevator doors opened and they stepped inside, the orderly said, "Floor, please?"

"All the way up." Angelo smiled with his mouth closed.

The orderly pressed the button with a flourish and they glided upward. At the second floor Lebedov got on, empty-handed; he looked lost without his cart.

"Third floor: baby clothes, toys, record players," the orderly intoned, holding his hand out protectively as the doors opened and closed again. Lebedov stared at him with his brooding eyes. His squat, powerful figure, even while it maintained its leaden, broken quality, seemed to lean forward; his lips moved slightly against each other, and his huge, stiff hands rubbed against his white trousers. The elevator ascended with a whining, cable-slapping sound, through a particularly strong smell of ether.

They all got out on the fifth floor. Lebedov shuffled off toward another wing, but the new orderly walked for a short way with Angelo; when they passed a statue of Jesus, he jerked his long colorless face at it and said in a whisper, "He work here?"

"Full time," said Angelo, and went on down the corridor.

But he felt a mild preoccupation as he handed the last of his ice cream and a movie magazine to a woman in a pink bed jacket, and in the next room he looked hard at the naked-faced man who lay there repeatedly belching and grimacing with pain. He paid Angelo for the carton of cigarettes and the bottle of witch hazel and, with an impatient wave of his hand, told him to keep the quarter change. And all the time he stared at the empty air between him and the crucifix with an expression of bewilderment; and whenever he belched, his fingers traced the course of his pain slowly up his chest.

After the last room, halting on the threshold of the lobby, Angelo tried to remember where he should have delivered the bottle of scented alcohol that remained in his carton. As he was consulting his list again, a nun rustled by, and he looked up to meet the frigid face of Sister Louise. Her eyes, through all the years he had been coming here, had known enough to condemn him as a natural enemy.

"Kindly do not leave that box there," she said. "Several times I've found your litter about the building." She spoke from a position of power; for more than a year she had been the temporary occupant of the ailing Mother Superior's chair, and there seemed no question that she would succeed the old woman. For the present, however, she still did not have the title, and Angelo guessed that this rankled in her.

"Okay, Sister," he said. "But that couldn't have been my litter, Sister. I'm very neat."

"Yesss, I'm *sure* you are," she said in a starchy voice. "See that you continue to be."

"Oh I *will*, Sister," he answered.

And then, as the sibilance of her garments blew past him into her office, he turned back to his list, wrinkling his nose unconsciously at the powdery intimation of scent she had left behind. His strip of paper was slashed with the rough lines of his crossings out. But there, near the bottom of the page, was one order, written very small and not checked off; Room 539 still waited for Frank's soothing lotion. Wearily he headed back upstairs.

The crumpled-faced little man reached through the side bars of his bed to pay him. When Angelo put his hand out for the money, the man seized it with hot, talon-like fingers.

"And what's *your* name, sonny?" he asked in a weak, phlegmy voice.

"Angelo, my name's Angelo." He looked over the wispy head with an expression that might have been exasperation if it had not been so controlled and familiar.

"And what grade are you in, Angelo?" the man asked, without relinquishing the hand; for him the difference between nine and nineteen was infinitesimal.

"I'm through with school. I work now and I got to get back to my job or I'll get fired." Angelo nodded toward his imprisoned hand.

"Oho! You're a restless one, aren't you?" the old man said slyly. "You don't like people to touch you. I know, I can tell. A lone wolf, hah? Well, don't be too sure of yourself. I was a lone wolf, too, but now I have to have my ass wiped by strangers. Echh . . ." The short sound of disgust seemed to light his eyes with a brief flame of pain and horror. Finally he looked up at the ceiling and said from the corner of his mouth, "Well, good luck to you, sonny."

"Sure, thanks. Okay, 'night, pop. I'll be around tomorrow if you want anything."

"If I *want* anything! Oh my, if I want anything . . ." He began to laugh, arching his body upward.

Angelo moved out into the corridor and cocked his head slightly, listening to the familiar medley of sounds. The furry voice of the loudspeaker called out over the muffled resonance of people's voices; here was the soft slap of cushioned shoes, there a muted radio, and all around was the enormous hum that filled the hospital interminably and certified its electric life. Glassware tinkled, metal struck metal in light ringings, someone laughed, and, more distantly, someone else cried.

The orderly's voice called softly from the darkened solarium. "Hey *boychik,* out here—come on."

Angelo narrowed his eyes and stepped forward cautiously. Variously shaped chairs and couches made dim, human forms, and the upper branches of a gigantic beech tree rustled with vague movement outside the windows. In one corner

34

he could just make out the seated white figure in the wheel-chair.

"Yeah, come on, don't be strange," the orderly said. "I took some tomatoes from the kitchen, some ginger ale. We'll have us a little *nosh*. Go ahead, sit, sit, I got two place settings." He waved toward another wheelchair.

"Well, I got to get back to the store," Angelo said half-heartedly. But he put his carton down and sat on the wheel-chair. Gradually he made out the small magazine table, upon which were three tomatoes, a salt shaker, and two bottles of soda complete with straws. He picked up one of the tomatoes and began polishing it against his shirt.

"When you start to work here?" he asked with bored courtesy. He took a bite of the tomato, and the taste reinforced the oddness he felt in being there. "I mean I never seen you around before."

"Yesterday." The orderly offered him a napkin. "I come to town yesterday with only five bucks in my pants and I said to myself, Sammy, you better get a job. So I come here and said to the Sister, I worked in a lot of hospitals and I'm very experienced. I could give references. I worked in Jewish hospitals, Catholic hospitals, Protestant hospitals, Quaker hospitals, not to mention nonsectarian. I'm hard-working and honest, respectful, *and* efficient. I'm Jewish, but I'm not pushy and not loud. On top of all, I work cheap. She's a hard woman, that Sister, but she knows a bargain—she hired me." He held his hands out palm up.

"Where'd you come from?"

"Oh, all over."

Angelo made a skeptical sound.

"New York?"

"Are you asking *me*?" Angelo said.

"How about you?" Sammy said.

"I always lived here."

"And you been working in that store a long time?"

"Yeah."

"Aha," Sammy said, nodding his long head as at a discovery. His hair was very fine and long, and in the dark it
was like a vapor. "And are you a good boy?" he asked.

"What're you talking about?"

"Do you honor your mother and father, and not steal, and
not covet your neighbor's wife? Or, on the other hand, are
you just a plain animal? Maybe you're *intelligent?*" He
leaned back and peered down his nose.

"Are you nuts?" But almost immediately Angelo's irritation turned into curious amusement. "Since you're giving
me a choice—say I'm intelligent. Go on, test me, ask a question."

"Okay. Tell me this: how did she have the baby if the
husband didn't *shtup* her?" He hunched himself like a chilled
stork and put his hands over his mouth to cover silent laughter. But Angelo began to laugh, too, rolling his head against
the wood and wicker back of the wheelchair.

He cut himself off at the sight of a white face that hung
in the doorway. Sister Louise hovered there for a minute,
her gaze avoiding them.

"Make sure that all the screens are latched," she said to
someone behind her. "There have been insects flying around."
And then she was gone. Angelo knew that she had seen them
there, but for some reason of her own she had preferred not
to acknowledge the fact.

"He did *shtup* her, *compa',*" Angelo said, still looking at
the doorway where the nun had stood. "That's no riddle."

"Aren't you a Catholic?" Sammy sounded disappointed.

"Sorry." Angelo finished the tomato and dabbed at the juice that ran down his chin. "I'm just a homo sapiens."

Suddenly Sammy began to sing in a high sweet voice:

> "I don't care if it rains or freezes,
> I am safe in the arms of Jesus.
> I am Jesus' little lamby,
> Yes, by Jesus Christ I amby."

"Hey, you just let that Sister Louise hear you and you'll be out on your ass so fast . . ." There seemed no conviction in Angelo's voice as he stared through the window at the whispering beech leaves. His eyes made out the stars all around the windowed room.

"But it don't bother *you*, hah?" Sammy asked. "That I make jokes like that?"

"Why do you want to get *me* sore?"

"Well, I tell you. That's how I make friends with people."

"You must be a regular Dale Carnegie."

"No, it's that I get them to really pay attention that way. See, when they're a little sore and curious, I can find out more about them. People have to get . . . well . . . Like you rub your skin against something rough—you know, scrape yourself. Your skin gets tender, you feel every little thing—a breeze, a little brushing against it." His white face was incredibly earnest. "It's like I can see their nerves. . . ."

"Uh-huh." This Hebe orderly, Angelo thought, another kook. Most of the orderlies he had known had something wrong with them. They were either crippled or old or colored or a little off in the head. In some cases, he guessed, the job made them that way. Or else it attracted that kind because it demanded no special skill or intelligence and there were always openings.

37

Sammy rubbed his face thoughtfully, shaping his features with long, sensitive-looking fingers. Crickets sent their songs in on a film of breeze. A bell rang somewhere deep in the building; a door slammed; someone distantly screamed. Angelo felt almost asleep, and jerked himself erect.

"Hey, I got to get back to the store." When he stood, the wheelchair rolled back a few inches, soundlessly. He stretched, and spoke from the shape of a yawn. "Maybe you better get your ass moving too, buddy. Sister Louise catches you and you're on unemployment."

"Ah, don't worry about me, I been around. In the meantime, good night, Angelo DeMarco."

Angelo waved negligently and went along the corridor to the elevator.

Back in the store, Frank asked what had kept him so long.

"Oh, I had a late supper with a friend. We got caught up in a discussion of philosophy, and then, what with the cigars and the brandy, we just lost track of time."

"You're real funny," Frank said. "But just don't forget what I'm paying you for."

"What you're barely paying me for."

"Anything I hate, it's a wise wop."

Angelo made an extravagantly obscene suggestion to Frank, who broke out in his maniacal laughter. But Angelo stared suddenly at the black windows of the store. A long, foolish face with great staring eyes seemed to float there, blurring his vision.

How did he know my name? he asked himself.

The question seemed far more important than the easy answers.

CHAPTER FOUR

THE sunlight fell in a morning slant on Theresa's head. She sat on a chair whose back had long ago broken off; Angelo stood beside her, showing with the language of his fingers how to use the small toy loom he had bought for her. She leaned into his voice, her eyes pinned on his dark fingers and the colored yarn that he was hooking on the rim of the loom, and after a while she moved her own fingers in a tentative attempt to match her brother's rhythm.

The air was cool and she wore a light sweater that bagged at the elbows; her hair was tied back in a ponytail with green ribbon. On all sides rose the wooden back porches that looked like fire escapes, but it was a high, clear morning, and the sun made the ailanthus leaves as haughty as elm foliage and, falling on the random litter of the yard, reflected from bits of glass that had lain there so long that their edges were rounded.

"See, now you push this one under and over that one. Under and over, under and over, under and over . . . all the way across. Now this one, the same thing, under and over, under and over. There, now you try it, come on, under and over, under and over. . . ."

Esther stood at the kitchen window watching them, her arms making a W under her breasts, one hand toying with the silver cross that hung there. And as though the guardian of reason agreed to turn away for a little while, she tried to make something sweet and pretty of her children. A brother and sister playing together, close, protective. The family that prays together, stays together. . . . And there were Mother-Daughter Dresses, Dad, Mom, Sugar-and-Spice. Ah, see Theresa in bridal white, standing beside a tall, faceless young Italian with clean hands and wavy hair. Esther herself was somewhat vague in old-blue lace and matching picture hat, but Angelo was clear and fine as he knelt devoutly, the colors of the stained-glass light covering him with a look of love and gentleness. The organ music swelled up from a sea-shell depth. . . . She was almost smiling when Angelo lifted his head and saw her. Theresa followed his hard gaze, forcing the mother back to her kitchen.

Her husband, Dante, had begged to use a prophylactic after Angelo, when the doctor had said she should not have another child. "What am I, a *puttan'*, that you should use *that?*" she had cried furiously. So they had had whatever Theresa was; and then, because she would not relent and they both knew they could not risk another such disaster, they had stopped being man and wife. She was so much a part of her vows that she could not risk even love. Murder to waste the seed, yet look at what she had now. Didn't she sin every living hour in not being able to love either of them in the way she should? *"Madre mia,* then what, *what?"* She crossed herself twice.

Outside, Angelo watched Theresa moving the strip of wool. "That's right, you're doing it right. Use any colors you want. See, there's yellow and red and blue. . . ." For a minute longer he watched the slow machine he had set in motion; then he walked over toward the cellar door where his book lay. "I got to go to work. Maybe you'll have a little rug by the time I get home."

But she stopped to watch him go, her eyes on him as he picked up the book, tucked it under his arm, and walked toward the alley. He turned at the corner of the house and signaled for her to continue weaving. She made no move to do so, and he went away in the face of her disobedience. He knew she would fix her eyes on the last place he had been visible to her, even long after he had gone out of sight.

Frank scowled at the bottle of syrup-of-figs. "Oh, say, Ange," he said. "My kid is having First Communion next week. The wife says tell Angelo to come. We figure to have a party after, you know. . . ."

Angelo shook his head without apology as he moved around the store with the feather duster. He slid out one of the triangular-seated chairs that fitted beneath the table like slices of pie, stood on it, and began dusting the big overhead fan.

"What'd you say?" Frank asked.

"You know what I said." Angelo brushed away a piece of dirt that had fallen on his face.

"Well, *why* not, Ange?"

Angelo looked down at him from the chair, one eyebrow

raised, his mouth curled slightly to one side. "Because I'm so crazy about churches and I'm so queer for priests that I'm afraid I'd get carried away from emotion and make a scene."

"All right, all right, be a wise guy. Cryin' out loud, I ain't asking you to take *vows!* You don't have to *do* anything there. It's a social occasion. You just come and watch, then we all go back to the house for food and *vino*. Nobody gonna bite you." His face took on an ingratiating expression and he spoke more softly. "And hey, my kid sister-in-law is gonna be there. You remember her, the little *braciol'* with the nice set of knockers. Maybe you'll work out something with her." Breathless with good will, he gazed up at Angelo.

Angelo shook his head slowly. "I just can't get over how important it is to you for me to come. It's very flattering," he said, without expression, getting down and sliding the chair back in place.

"Well, I tell you, Ange," Frank said with a faraway look, his voice down a few tender notes. "You know how close I was with Dante, your old man. I mean we were more like brothers than cousins. Oh I could tell you stories of the times we had . . ." He sighed noisily. "Eh, what's the use talking, water over the dam. But the thing is, it makes me feel close to you," he said intensely. "It's like you was my own son or . . ."

"You're so full of shit, it's funny," Angelo said with a grin. "You insult my intelligence. Why, you *citrull'*, do you think I was born yesterday? The thing is, you made a bet with yourself, or your wife, or Dominic, or someone. You said, 'I bet I can work that kid into the fold—it just takes patience and brains.' I don't say you care whether my soul is saved, only you figure it for a sort of challenge, a little exercise for that twisted brain you got."

"I never saw nothing like it!" Frank held his hands out in

an appeal of innocence. "I just give a nice, generous invitation and I get insulted like I did a crime. Aw, you're in a bad way, Angelo, a real bad way. Okay, okay, *don't* come. Go around like a mad dog biting the hand that feeds you. Honest to God, I never seen . . ."

"But what I don't understand," Angelo said, going behind the counter, where he began to replenish the cigarette bins, "is how someone with such a sly, scheming brain like you could swallow all the garbage the priests feed you."

"You don't understand nothing, Angelo," Frank said sadly, shaking his head. "You're immature is what you are. You're not flexible. Everything got to be black or white with you. Listen, you got to ride with things, accept things. There's good things in the Church, there's stupid. If you're smart you take what you need. Take me, for instance, the Church don't hamper me at all. I figure, if God is so wise, He must expect a little cutting of corners. He knows human beings are weak. And *I* know that *He* knows, so what I got to worry about?"

Angelo sighed admiringly. "I got to admit, Frank, you *do* have it knocked up. I got to hand it to you. Too bad my mother isn't as reasonable as you."

"So don't it make sense to you?"

Angelo shook his head.

"And you won't come to my party?"

Angelo continued shaking his head.

Frank stared at him and felt his irritation flower into spite; he looked around for something with which to punish his employee. His glance fell on the clock and he grinned, knowing Angelo's special bane. "Okay, enough socializing, back to business. It's two thirty, *paesan'*, time for the hospital. Hit the road."

To his disappointment, Angelo seemed oddly cheerful about

43

going. Frank watched him tear off the strip of paper, flip a pencil in the air and catch it, and walk out swiftly. He went to the door and gazed after him. He could never figure that kid out. Maybe Angelo was a genius. The idea tossed in his head for a moment like a sad note. Then, unable to support melancholy among the manipulations of his mind, he went into the back room to concoct some more DeMay products.

Angelo cut through the bright afternoon, breathing a queer expectancy, and for some reason he started with the children's pavilion. A little sun-blinded, he went inside and started down the row of beds, to begin at the far end.

He was halfway along when the orderly's figure appeared through the sun spirals. Sammy was leaning over Maria Alvarez, talking softly and intently, his face extraordinarily pale and hazy beside her dark skin. Angelo felt a faint uneasiness and stopped at the foot of the bed.

"We were just playing a game," Sammy explained without smiling. "Ghost—it's a spelling game. But I don't think she plays fair. I think she makes words up." He looked at the child suspiciously; there was no trace of condescending humor on his face. Maria just shook her head with a stubborn expression. "She didn't even have a 'G' and I got a whole 'Ghost.' I shouldn't play without I have a dictionary. I mean, for example, Angelo, serious, there's no such word as *marlevoude,* is there?"

Angelo shrugged. "Maybe in Puerto Rican. Ask her if it's in Puerto Rican."

"Supposed to be only American," Sammy said.

Maria just pressed her lips together smugly.

"You better give it up," Angelo said. "She's probably too educated for you."

"Next time I wouldn't play without a dictionary." Sammy turned and walked away on his stilt legs, and Maria looked raptly after him.

"Want anything today?" Angelo asked, watching the long figure disappear out the door. When he looked back at her, she was printing laboriously. Finally she held it up to him.

Her note read, "I DONT HAVE MUNY TODAY."

"You can pay me tomorrow if you promise to get money from your mother when she comes," he offered. "I'll trust you for a cup of ice cream."

Her hair lay like a black satin scarf on the pillowcase and she gazed at him without blinking. Until last night he had never noticed the hissing that came from the disk at her throat.

She took up her pencil again and wrote another note.

"WHAT IF I DONT PAYE YOU TUMORROW ETHER?"

"I don't see how you could have beat him in a spelling game," he muttered. "Oh, well, I just wouldn't trust you again. You'd ruin your credit. Maybe I'd even have you put in debtors' prison."

She made a sour face for his meaningless talk.

He crumpled her note and threw it onto her bed. "Vanilla?" he asked, pencil to paper.

She nodded without looking at him and began fussing with the Negro doll.

Horace Weingarden, the boy with the delicate face and thick lips, ordered a chocolate soda; Virginia Lindstrom, the blonde with the bandaged eyes, asked for ice cream. He wrote everything down.

In the main building, Howard Miller ordered a sandwich. He stood in his specially bought, rather feminine nylon uniform, watching Angelo; his face twitched constantly, his mouth moving, brow furrowing and unfurrowing. He had made overtures to Angelo in the past, but now wondered what could have attracted him in that battered, lean boy.

On the fifth floor Sullivan drew him into an alcove, where she ordered a box of Kotex and watched him with a curious and taunting expression. "You're a funny kid," she said finally, when he looked up at her without embarrassment. She leaned against the wall, her arms folded, her triangular eyes squinting. "I mean, a while ago I was in a store ordering a box of Kotex, and the kid there, about your age, got red in the face and fell all over himself from embarrassment. He couldn't even look me in the eye, but you . . ."

"You get embarrassed from surprise, when you're off balance or mixed up. Nothing to get embarrassed about. I know women menstruate and Kotex absorbs the blood." He held his hands out, obviously rational.

Sullivan flushed and her smile became fixed. "You're a cool cookie, Angelo, but sometimes you . . . you bother me."

"What do you want, I should act like that kid you were talking about? Okay, just to make you feel better. How's this?" he tucked his head shyly into his shoulder and, casting his eyes downward, began to scuff the floor with his toe. "Aw, shucks, Miss Sullivan, gosh, gee . . ."

"You little louse." Sullivan began to laugh. "I give up. You're too much for me."

"How do you know, you haven't tried me," he said with a leer.

"All right, that's enough," she said, still smiling, but from within a wrapping of severity. "Now you look and sound like the other Wooster Street dagoes."

"Oh Sister!" he exclaimed with amused scorn.

Sullivan pinched his arm, her expression both scowl and smile; she really didn't know what she thought of him. She stalked out of the alcove, her uniform rustling, a scent of Lifebuoy in her wake. Angelo shook his head, stared after her for a minute or two, stepped out into the corridor, and went on with his rounds.

Nearing the emergency entrance, on his way back to the

store, he heard a cabinet door slam shut. The sound seemed to come from the emergency room, but when he reached the doorway, he saw Sammy swabbing the floor, which was covered with water. Sammy seemed to notice him from the corner of his eye and began to mop with a slow, almost dreamy motion. After a few seconds he turned the mop upside down, seized the mop handle close to his body, and began waltzing slowly with it, an entranced expression on his face. His feet made sloshing sounds in the inch of water on the floor and he crooned softly. There was an awkward bulge in his rear pants pocket.

"You don't show the right respect for your job," Angelo said. "They don't like for you not to have a reverent attitude."

Sammy looked up in feigned surprise. "Oh gee, Angelo! You scared me. What's that, *boychik,* not reverent? No, no, just the opposite, just the opposite. In fact I was acting out one of the miracles."

"Which one was that?"

Sammy lifted one foot, splashed it down, then did the same with the other. "What else?" he said. "Walking on the water."

Angelo grimaced. "I don't care what you were doing, but don't ever try to pull the wool over *my* eyes. For the record, I figure you were doing something you shouldn't be doing just before I got here." He smiled coldly.

Another kind of smile folded the skin beneath Sammy's eyes. "Oh, I can see you're smart. You got everything figured, hah?" His voice seemed to hold several layers of feeling: tenderness, cruelty, humor, and something else that Angelo could not identify. Suddenly his face went simple again—simple, that is, in its own queer determined way. "But why do you say that? What makes you think I was doing something not kosher?"

47

"Your face was like a kid getting caught at the cooky jar."

"A cooky jar." Sammy shook his head admiringly. "You're a regular Hawkshaw, Angelo. Imagine, a *cooky jar* . . ."

Something chafed Angelo and a retort came to his mouth. But he saw its childishness just in time. The fact was, he realized, Sammy was teasing him. What do I have to prove? The guy is a nut, that's all.

"Looky, looky, looky, here comes Cooky, walking down the street. . . ."

Sammy sang it at him, but Angelo regained his sense of humor and grinned. It was all right, but one of these days he might have to get something on this clown, just to straighten out the pecking order for him.

CHAPTER FIVE

ON Angelo's evening trip the following Monday Sammy stopped him and said there was a patient in the alcove along the corridor waiting to be moved to another room. "He says he wants to order a few things; you should wake him if he's sleeping. It's the old cocker from 539; they're getting another room ready."

Angelo plodded on, feeling drained and tired. It was hot, and there were few visitors, so the building was abnormally quiet. The evening glowed like a mass of embers in the window of each room he passed; against that swooning brilliance, the figures of the patients were obscure and dark. He found himself longing with disproportionate intensity for an icy bath that might end his lassitude.

When he came to the alcove, it glowed like the interior of a furnace. Subdued voices from the next room seemed to charge the fiery sunset light. The wheeled stretcher stood against the orange-lit wall, and the old man lay sleeping comfortably, his face up toward the ceiling.

"DeMarco's Pharmacy. You want to order anything? Ice cream, alcohol, candy, cigarettes, stationery, shaving cream?" At each item he raised his voice a little more and stepped closer. "Hey, pop, you told the orderly you wanted something. How about it?" He shook the frail shoulder and talked on although he began to know what was wrong. "I mean we got forceps, dextri-maltose, disposable diapers, combs and toothpaste, liquor, tobacco, all-purpose vitamins. Name it, we got it: condoms, suppositories, chewing gum, talcum, diaphragms, magazines, cameras, clocks. There's trusses and corn pads, sandwiches, laxatives, candy, aspirin. . . ."

Laughter came from the doorway.

"Okay already, *bubi,* don't be dense," Sammy said. "You know he's not gonna wake up. It's a joke."

Angelo slowly took his hand from the body. "Oh crap," he said in a mild voice. "What gets me is that I knew it all along. That's what gets me."

"That was a good one, wasn't it, *boychik?*"

"Oh, it was a dilly. You're a comedian of a very high order."

"I got a million jokes," Sammy acknowledged.

"I just bet you have," Angelo said. Then he began to shudder, so that the strip of paper in his hand rattled; he tried to control the shuddering by making his body rigid. Another stiff, he told himself, that was all. He had seen dozens in the years he had been coming to the hospital, and though he had not ever touched one before, he knew that there was nothing in death that frightened him. The thing was, he

50

knew the body, from skull to phalanges, from the epidermis in. The heart was a large muscle pump that nourished the body with blood. And when everything stopped, there was merely rubbish. Yet his body continued to vibrate and the paper rustled in his fingers.

"Boy, how do you like this," he said. "I'm in great shape, hah?"

Sammy walked over to him, still smiling. He put his hand on Angelo's arm. "But you're so *tough*, Angelo. You're a tough, tough *luksh*," he said tenderly. "I can play tricks on you and not worry you'll get upset, hah, *boychik?*"

Angelo's body stopped trembling, at last, and he looked toward the corpse. "I ought to bust you right in the mouth. That'd be the best thing."

"But we're friends," Sammy objected.

"How the hell you figure that?"

"Well, I give you food and we talk," Sammy said, holding his hands out.

"Hey, I don't know what kind of nut you are, buddy," Angelo said, quite remote from anger. "But you're asking for trouble with all your screwing around. You got some kind of deal you're pulling—okay, that's your business. But I got work to do. Friend like you and a guy don't need an enemy. Why don't you just shuffle off and leave me be, hah? This job breaks my hump as it is—I don't *need* you."

"Ah, he's tired," Sammy said with exaggerated compassion.

Angelo still hadn't moved, and the light had receded quite suddenly as the sun dipped beneath the trees and rooftops outside. The two living figures and the dead one were all dim, and when the lights flicked on in the corridor outside the alcove, they fell into contrasting darkness.

"Yeah, you're tired," Sammy said. "Young kid like you, working all hours. It's not right. . . ."

"Save it, will ya. I'm nineteen."

51

"Nineteen! My, my, practically an old man."

"Look, what do you want?"

"Want? Want? *Nothing*. Go, go, write down, bring the merchandise back. After, I'll meet you in the solarium. We'll break a little bread *efsher?*"

Angelo peered at him fiercely, trying to discern his motives in the darkness. But there was just his vague length and the dim absurdity of his face.

"Okay, okay," he said, his voice rising slightly, and he turned away.

As he worked his way down the ward, delivering to the children, he looked over from time to time to where Sammy made shadow figures on the wall beside Maria's bed. The bony body was hunched and the fingers were interlaced; when Angelo came closer he heard the high, soft voice, delicate as a tungsten wire.

"Here's an ostrich. And a dog—see his mouth open and close, and his tongue, *err-raughh!* And look here at this, what's this, hah? A *snake*—can't you tell it's a snake? Now, wait a minute. . . . A rabbit—see his ears. And now look here, see the thing-a-jig, the comb, yeah, yeah, a rooster. And how's this—a *faird*, a horse . . ."

An angry voice intruded.

"What do you think you're doing, orderly?" Sister Mary Frances said. She stood with her hands on her hips, her football-player face comically belligerent as she blocked Sammy's exit from between the beds. "Are you supposed to be doing some work here? If so, get to it and leave the children alone. They should be sleeping anyhow. It's bad enough we allow *other* privileges." She looked significantly at Angelo.

"Ah, sure, and I was jist after jollyin' the wee one, Sister. The wee colleen needs a bit o' cheerin' up, you know,"

Sammy said with a charming smile. And then, as though in afterthought, "Begorra."

Sister Mary Frances stared incredulously. "Yes, all well and good," she said feebly. "But still . . ."

"I'll be on my way then, Sister. May the saints preserve ye." He edged past her so close that she was forced to sit heavily on Maria's bed.

Angelo had to cough to restrain the giggle in his throat, and some of the children stirred restlessly around them.

"Isn't *he* the queer one?" Sister Mary Frances said as she rose.

Angelo shrugged and glanced through the ward; Sammy had disappeared.

He gave Maria her ice cream, and she looked at him with a malicious smile when he reminded her that she owed him for two days' refreshments. "If you don't pay me tomorrow . . ." He made a cutting motion across his throat.

"YOU WOOD NOT DO ANYTHING ANYWAYS," her note taunted.

"That's what you think. I'm a Sicilian, we're knifers."

"YUR MEAN TO CHILDRIN," the block letters concluded.

"I'm mean to everyone," he called back over his shoulder as he headed for the door. The nun hissed for quiet, and he held up his hand in acknowledgment.

When he had finished his deliveries and looked into the fifth-floor solarium, Lebedov and Howard Miller were there with Sammy, who was lighting a votive candle in the center of a low round table.

"I didn't know it was gonna be formal," Angelo said.

"I'm celebrating my birthday," Sammy explained.

"How old are you?"

"Ah, that would be telling."

Angelo sat on the couch and watched the candlelight flicker over the three orderlies' faces. Howard's writhed as usual;

Lebedov looked like a ragged old beast, surprised and uncertain before the tiny flame. Sammy waved munificently at the sandwiches piled on the brown hospital tray. *"Ess, fress, kinder."*

"Oh, but you're old *enough,* aren't you, Sammy dear?" Howard said.

"Yeah, *faygele,* I'm old enough for anything."

"I tell you," Lebedov grunted. "I sixty year old my own self."

"Your *own* self—amazing!" Howard said distastefully. "You don't look a day over fifty-nine."

"I strong like a ox," Lebedov said. "Since I'm boy, always strong. Work since five year old, don't have what to eat, live in shed with holes in roof. Two brothers, they die. Not me! I strong like ox." He filled his chest and let the air out slowly, demonstrating his capacity. "Yeah, brothers die that time. Priest come around, says pray. Not me, hah, I know. Shit, burn damn church with priest altogether. What they do for Lebedov, hah?"

"Man after my own heart," Angelo said. "Regular old freethinker, ain't you, Lebedov?"

"But I bet he *was* a real bull when he was young," Howard said wistfully, staring at the powerful wreck of the old man's body.

"Could use to bend iron bar." Lebedov looked with revulsion at his huge, cumbersome hands. "Not no more."

"Hey, Lebedov, you kill many Jews over there in Roosia?" Sammy asked.

"I never do that stuff. Them animals get excite in church, go out on Easter drunk. Not that shit for Lebedov. Lebedov like to be alone. Walk in field on Sunday, look at pretty flowers, butterfly. Them butterfly . . ." He licked his torn mouth; his eyes kindled. "What pretty color—purple, yellow

. . . I always try to catch him, hold him. Every time though, get all squash. Try to hold him easy, but he get squash. Echh! Same like womans—see him faraways, look so pretty, get him. Echh, no damn good."

"I think you're mixing up your sexes," Angelo said from around the straws.

"Sexis?" Lebedov said stupidly.

"Leave him alone," Howard said. "I'm all for that kind of mix-up."

For a while they sat eating and drinking in silence. In the candlelight, the walls appeared insubstantial, like paper partitions shaking in a wind. From down the hall, the quiet resonance of the loudspeaker carried the calls; outside the screened windows, the huge old beech tree stood motionless.

Angelo fixed hard on what *was,* and stared at the beacon light on the new building, seeing faintly its immense, pale shape against the dark sky.

"It looks like a tombstone or a factory," Sammy said, following his gaze. "Too cold-looking, got no character."

"Maybe for you," Angelo replied. "Maybe you like dark corners, maybe you're sneaky—you got angles. You wouldn't have a chance under fluorescents."

"What angles?" Sammy said evenly. "I do my work, make my modest salary. . . . I wonder, though. Do you really think people will be better off there?"

"Sure, why shouldn't they? It'll be more efficient, they'll have better equipment."

"But it's so impersonal," Sammy insisted.

"What do you want—it's a *hospital!*"

Sammy sat back and squinted through the candlelight at him. "You know, you shoulda been a scientist, Angelo. I got to admire how clear-cut you see things. Yeah, a regular scientist . . ."

"And what's wrong with that?"

"Yeah, but *bubele,* what do the scientists know about *love?*" Sammy said crooningly, his face benign, drowsy, and shining.

"Yes, dearie, *love,*" Howard echoed with wistful lewdness.

"They know. And they know about the crap people surround themselves with, why they need words like that. They know about the things people are afraid of and the things they invent to cover themselves."

"So it's all a bunch of *buhba meisse* then?" Sammy asked humbly.

"Whatever that means."

"Now, how do you like that? I didn't even know," Sammy said with an amazed expression. "Such crazy things! It's encouraging that there's good solid answers, I kid you not. I mean like the time I seen a skinny little guy hold five guys on his chest while he was laying between two chairs. . . ."

"Hypnotic suggestion," Angelo said.

"Sure, of course. I'll have to get you to explain a lot of things for me, *bubi.* Like another time, I seen a dog letting a cat suck its titties. . . ."

"It's common." Angelo began to feel slightly apprehensive about the dim shape of Sammy's humor.

"Out west once, I heard a guy sing so beautiful that people couldn't move, actually couldn't *move!*" He held his hand up before Angelo could comment. "I know, I know. But in Chicago, I seen a butcher cut up his wife in his refrigerator and then kiss her all over when she was dead. The funny thing there was that he looked happier than anyone I ever saw. Oh, and wait. In Springfield there was a terrific fire in a orphanage, and a guy went in and out, bringing out the kids, with his own clothes on fire. His whole body got burned to a crisp, but he kept on going and bringing them out. When the last kid was out, he said, 'Well, that's all of 'em.' Then he dropped dead. No, no, wait," he said, forestalling Angelo's silent objection.

"One winter I was in Duluth," he went on quickly. "And there was this rich kid there named Terry something—I forget. Good-looking, nice-built kid, had everything. He used to hang around the hospital, thought he might be a doctor or like that. We used to kibitz around a little, you know. Anyhow, one day I'm walking with him and we see this ugly, blind dwarf tapping along the street with a cane. Terry looked kind of disgusted, but he goes over and helps the dwarf across the street, holding the dwarf's arm like it was a piece of *dreck*, like it was making him sick to his stomach. I mean, that dwarf was pretty horrible-looking, like something in a funhouse mirror. Well, Terry walks him another block, and when he gets to the corner, I guess he didn't let the dwarf know they had got to the curb, and the dwarf falls over. He fell kind of strange—soft and crazy like in a nightmare. He looked like one of those toys that if you knock them over they rock right back. But he didn't, just lay there like he's swimming. Terry stares at him, and I never seen such a look in anyone's eyes—sick, frightened, or something else, I don't know. Finally he helped the dwarf up, and the dwarf looked at him with them blind eyes, not saying a word. This Terry just began to shake, and then he took the dwarf's arm and led him off again. I don't know what happened, but after that I used to see that rich, good-looking kid leading the dwarf around all the time, and all the time he looked just as disgusted and sick. . . . Then I was down in Albuquerque one springtime . . ."

Angelo sat there, stunned and breathless, pinned to the couch by the high, insistent voice. There was no break in the narratives. Sammy turned from one to another of them, waving his long fingers expressively, now widening his eyes, now narrowing them, interrupting himself, piling story upon story, leading his listeners' attention as a conductor leads musicians.

". . . a tree growing right out of rock, no dirt or nothing. Can you figure? And that same month I went to this place where they had a stream that flowed uphill, so help me, *uphill!* It was like in a damn fun house. That darn water just . . ."

Lebedov sat nodding and moving his hands. His bestial face was animated; his eyes gleamed. He licked his lips and leaned forward as though ready to interrupt at any time. Howard Miller's face stopped twitching, became almost sleepy and still.

". . . and there was a horse that raped a woman and she got pregnant. You could imagine the tumult, because she came from a very Orthodox . . ."

And Angelo sat there, appalled at his helplessness, struggling against it, until rage got him to his feet. "All right. What are you trying to prove with that shit?"

"Prove, prove?" Sammy shrugged. "Nothing, *bubi,* nothing at all. Only that the world is round, that your neighbor's yard always looks like it got more chlorophyll, that everything is nothing, that you're right, Angelo, *absolutely right.*"

"I gotta go," Angelo said.

"Sleep well, *totinka.* Have pleasant dreams, *scientist.* Wake up bright."

"Fa'n cul' la madre," Angelo called back without feeling.

Walking down the corridor, he heard a patient howl Sammy's name with some attempt at secretiveness. Then he heard the high voice answer with a queer, amused-sounding tenderness. "Okay, friend, it's all right, Sammy's coming. Shhh, not so loud . . ."

And Angelo walked from the hospital into a night that seemed like a dream.

CHAPTER SIX

HE began to watch the orderly. Sometimes he pretended to leave the building but would really duck into an alcove or an empty room and, through a crack in a doorway, would watch the skinny figure bent enigmatically over a patient. Yet he never saw anything unusual take place. He watched Sammy help patients with bedpans, sit them up and lay them down, bring them beverages and food, change nightshirts and linens, and all with the solemn frivolity of a child playing with dolls.

Sometimes he came upon the patients in the act of calling for Sammy; more often he caught them just after Sammy had left, and surprised a mysterious yearning on their faces. A need was revealed in them: it almost appeared to be love.

When Angelo found even his waking hours at home haunted by thoughts of Sammy, he began to accept the fact that he was taking the conflict seriously. Somehow the man *had* gotten to him; whether or not he intended his odd performance explicitly for Angelo no longer seemed important. The thing was, Angelo lacked a social life, lacked anything to distract him from the intangible challenge Sammy seemed to have thrown down.

The city fell into a heat wave that broke old records. For a while Angelo was almost able to use the heat as an explanation for his strange state. He could hardly read; after a page or two he would sit staring at nothing, and would mutter at large, "I can't concentrate." And in the back yard he would look at his sister and experience the pain of bafflement, suffering at the sight of her pale, secretive face, which blurred in the suffocating evening like a strange white flower. Worst of all were his hospital encounters with Sammy. In spite of himself he was fascinated by the apparent irrationality of the man, and at the thought of seeing him he felt almost sick with anticipation.

In the sweltering air, he wore his routes into deeper grooves: the blocks to the store, the short walk to the hospital, the labyrinthine journeys through the huge building.

The patients lay like suffocating fish, their mouths open, their faces aimed toward the fraudulent promise of the outdoors. The children moaned and cried more weakly, or just lay with toys forgotten in their hands, gazing apathetically at the floor fan far down the ward. Constantly wet and softened by sweat, Angelo's list was smudged with his impatient scrawling. His cheeks and forehead streaked with graphite smudges from his fingers, he roamed among the ailing with a predatory expression.

And then the late evenings would come, and he would be stretched out on a wheelchair or a couch in the darkened solarium, sipping an icy soda and listening to Sammy's crazy reminiscences. Often Lebedov was there, growling irrelevant agreement and waving his cruel, powerful hands, stirred by Sammy's random narratives to an obscure excitement. Howard Miller, when he was present, would be less animated; he came, perhaps, only because the little nightly suppers provided, in his lonely world, a sort of stage upon which he could at least be seen and reacted to.

Even at those hours of the night the heat was heavy and maddening. Angelo would shift in his seat, wiping at the surface of his skin, hopeless of relief. His eyes would hang on Sammy's bloodless, hook-nosed face; yet what could be seen there? The head might tilt back and the eyes squint slightly as though peering through a wise-guy angle of cigarette smoke, and Sammy would be the personification of the lounging sidewalk superintendent in front of the kosher delicatessen. Or, letting his head droop to one side, he would become Hebraically weary. Or he might look up from under his large eyelids, humorous, melancholy, cynical, yet innocent too; perhaps worse than innocent, as though a prodigious weight of evil compressed something unbearable in him to a diamond-hard brilliance. The stories he told had no apparent pattern, were horrible and funny, sad and obscene. They jerked Angelo up with sudden changes of pace and mood, and were endlessly hypnotic just because of their total irrelevance to each other.

Often on such nights Angelo would catch a glimpse of Sister Louise in the corridor, at the edge of earshot, her face revealing the fearful hostility of the uninvited. Oddly, she never exercised her prerogative of censure. They didn't belong there, had no right to use the windowed porch for their shabby, private visiting and eating. Yet she did and said nothing.

The peak of the heat came on a Wednesday. The temperature didn't drop under a hundred until ten o'clock that night. When Angelo got to the solarium, the three orderlies were already there. He dropped into the wheelchair as though pushed, dizzy and half sick from the long day spent running around in the heat, and picked up one of the plums that lay among crescents of cantaloupe on the hospital tray. The plum burst under his teeth, and the sensation of wetness and sweetness was so intense that he shut his eyes for a moment. He ate slowly, concentrating on the rhythm of Sammy's story like a child trying to board a moving merry-go-round.

The other two orderlies sat motionless, almost rigidly attentive. Even the troubled sounds from the wards were absent, as though the heat had killed the patients. Nothing could be heard except the soft, thumping drone of the ventilator downstairs, and Sammy's voice.

". . . so this SS trooper comes up to my artist friend and says to him, 'Jew, I'll get you an extra bread ration and you will make a large crayon drawing from this snapshot of my girl friend. I'll pick it up in a few days.' Well, my friend goes into this little room he had in the barracks, and he makes this drawing and puts it behind this little glass door where the electric wires or telephone wires had a junction or something. Hardly anybody went there, and he figured it would stay neat and clean there. Well, my friend who was a Jewish guy kind of forgets about it after a few days. Then one day, this other German soldier who was an electrician comes in and asks where the junction box is. My friend, who had forgot the picture was there—not that he would have worried about it anyhow, because after all it was for an SS guy—takes the soldier very respectfully over to the junction box. The soldier-electrician opens the door and, almost with the same movement, swings around and clouts my friend on the nose so he falls down spouting blood from his nostrils. 'Hey, you rotten Jew, where'd you get this picture of my wife?' he screams. His *wife*! My friend just sat there on the floor, licking his own blood and staring up at the guy, kind of in shock, wondering how he could have got involved in a crazy coincidence like that. But after what he'd been through there, it didn't take him long to accept it. He figures, 'What the hell!' And he tells the soldier it was Obersturmführer So-and-so who gave him the picture. The soldier storms out of there, and my friend sat there on the floor amusing himself with the bright red blood on his fingers, until pretty soon two sets of feet come clomping down the hall. The soldier comes in with the SS man who had given my friend the picture, and he says, excited, 'Is this the guy that gave you the picture? You *did* say Obersturmführer So-and-so, didn't you?' But before my friend can focus on him, the SS guy yells, 'Did you tell him that I gave you that picture?' And both of them stand there glaring bloody murder at him, both getting redder and redder, so he felt they would blow him up any second. If he corroborates *anything*, he's calling one of them a liar. Well, you can imagine! My friend says he looked from one to the other, all the time saying to himself, 'Curse my mother, curse my father, curse my maternal grandparents, curse my paternal grandparents, curse their parents and their parents. . . .' All the way back to Adam, he cursed everybody who was responsible for him getting born. But just when he was going eeny meeny miney mo to pick which one should murder him, the SS guy suddenly remembers that he's more elite and special. He throws his chest out and says, 'All right, so *what* if she prefers me to you! What are you going to do about it?' Before you know it, they're screaming at each other and the next thing they're making with the hands. My friend just sneaked out quiet and never saw either one of them again. Of course, he never did get that extra bread the SS guy promised. Isn't that a yuck for you?"

Sammy paused only briefly, and was off again.

"In Rochester (just to show you how the end got nothing to do with the beginning) I lived in a boardinghouse with this pervert who was hot for little kids. (No offense meant, Howard.) No, but he was very pleasant and I don't know if he ever actually made out completely with any kid, but he sure was always looking. He was a fat guy with a big purple mark on his cheek and two fingers missing on his left hand. His mouth had a kind of nasty shape, but his eyes . . . well, his eyes were like weird. I don't know how to describe . . . like they seemed surprised to find themselves in that kind of face, like the eyes of somebody always waking up from a bad dream. Anyhow, this guy used to work at different crummy jobs—messenger, dishwasher, snow shoveler, you know. I even got him a job in the hospital I was in, but he quit at Christmas time to get a job as a department store Santa Claus, because he figured it was a chance to cop cheap feels from the kids who sat on his lap to ask him for the moon. One night I was in his room talking about literature or something. It was getting near spring then. He used to get real *nujy* in spring. He interrupted me and began talking about suicide like some people talk about some movie they plan to see. He favored cutting wrists but didn't altogether eliminate sleeping pills. Gas was out because we didn't have any, and he wouldn't jump from a building, he said, because he was afraid of heights. Well, just in the middle of his talk, the landlady comes in, sits on his bed, and begins crying. I don't know her well, so I keep quiet, but he says, 'What's the matter, Rena, why are you crying?' She tells him that her little girl needs her eyes operated on, and they have to get the eyes or parts of the eyes from someone and they don't know who. The fat guy stares at her for a long time until you can tell he don't even see her any more. Then he begins looking out the window at the leaves and he keeps doing that. The landlady stops crying and watches him. I just sit. After a long time, maybe a half hour, he turns back, not to her but to me, and when he speaks it's like he was continuing the talk he was making before she came in. 'So I'll just give her my eyes, that's all. I never read or go to the movies anyhow, and I've seen everything at least a dozen times already. Tell the doctor that, tell him we'll use my eyes—if they'll fit. After all, she has a small face. . . .' Well, believe it or not, he went through with it. They did the operations and the fat guy comes out of the hospital blind. They got him a white cane and a dog, and he used to stand on a street corner with a cup full of pencils, trying to touch the young kids when he heard their voices. It didn't seem to bother him to be blind, either. In fact he said to me once, the last time I saw him, that he didn't get restless any more. And you know, I believe it, because his eyes, or what was left there, seemed to belong to his face then."

Before Angelo could ask the obvious questions that would have exposed the outrageous story, Sammy was off on still another, leaving the last word of each tale hanging up in the air, thus beguiling his listeners into waiting for an ending that would never come.

"Because just about that time there was this dope peddler named Irving Sterling. He had the pot market sewed up in all the high schools and did a little special business with special clients for heroin, mostly with the local tarts. Irving was very efficient and conservative and he despised hoodlums and gangsters. He kept books and everything, and he was the only pusher I ever saw who extended credit for ninety days. I don't know how he stayed out of trouble with the cops, because he was too cheap to pay bribery. Maybe it was partly because he didn't *look* like a crook. He wore dark, cheap suits and had this meeky white face like a minister. But then, nothing is like it looks, is it? What I'm saying, to make a long story short, is that one night this tart named Violet was cutting across a lot where there was some construction going on, and this girder fell and pinned her leg somehow. Some cops came and a big crowd gathered, making clouds with their breath in the dark. The fire department came, and them and the cops stood around for a while, trying to figure out how to get her loose. She was bawling from pain. All of a sudden, Irving steps out of the crowd, his eyes fierce. He goes over to where the whore is laying on the ground. The cops asked what he wanted and he said he had an interest in her, patting his breast pocket, where I know he kept his account book. The cops shrugged and let him stay. Pretty soon a couple internes come up and begin looking her over and taking her pulse. Irving found a spot in the rubble and sat next to her. It began to sleet and rain and the water froze on the iron girder. The firemen began to cut the girder with an acetylene torch. The light from it made them all look funny, Irving and Violet and the firemen and cops and the whole crowd—like wood carvings. I called out to Irving and asked what he was doing there, and he answered that he was watching his investment, that she was in to him for two hundred and fifteen dollars and that he wasn't about to let her out of his sight. And then I noticed something that made me do a double take, and for a minute I thought it was because of that flickering light from the torch: Irving was holding her *hand!* She was whimpering with pain, her face was all twisted, and her dyed red hair looked like rusty Brillo; Irving just sat there, not saying a word to her but holding her hand while the sleet covered the two of them like frosting—they gleamed. I said, 'But, Irving, why do you have to hold her hand?' And he just said, 'When someone is in to you for all that money, it don't pay to take chances.' That's all, that's all he said. The hours went by and it got colder. Him and the tart looked like ice sculptures that they make for fancy parties. People brought them coffee, and Irving drank his and smoked his old pipe, but all with one hand because he wouldn't let go. They covered Violet with a blanket, she shouldn't freeze to death, and most of the people drifted away. I went into a diner across the street for a while to warm up and I watched through the window. They were lit up by a search light and that acetylene torch. You know, they looked like those Christmas scenes—very peaceful and nice. I went back over there and watched from up close. About three in the morning I said, 'But really, Irving, why are you freezing your balls? She's not going to go nowhere. Why *are* you sitting like that holding her hand?' And he turned to me, real stiffly, half froze already, and he said, 'Because she's gonna die, and she shouldn't die without anyone who knows her to hold her hand—I know that's the thing *I'm* most afraid of myself.' So he sat there and pretty soon it began to come morning and he looked like silver. But here's the pay-off. About six o'clock in the morning they got her loose and she was not in too bad a shape considering. Only they couldn't get Irving's hand off hers for a while, because *he* was dead, and his face had streaks of ice running down from the eyes. . . ."

And the three listeners were like addicts. He seemed to gloat quietly over them, looking longest at Angelo's face, proudest perhaps of *his* stupefaction; his expression said that the other two orderlies were typical material but that Angelo was a rarer trophy. And confident now in manner, he could even dare a minute or two of silence, like a lion tamer who puts down his whip and arrogantly turns his back upon the animals. Nothing broke from Angelo's mouth; in the prodigious heat, a painful pressure built up inside him. Distant crickets made a dreamlike whirring, a glassy ringing like the sound one hears when undergoing an anesthetic.

"Later on, this same tart, Violet," Sammy resumed in a slow, goading voice, "moved to Troy with her kid. She had a slight limp and a bad scar on her leg, but that didn't affect her business. Her kid, a tall skinny boy with a funny face who knew the score from the cradle, used to pimp for her. It was a mother-and-son business, you might say. No nonsense about them, both was strictly business. But one thing: come Mother's Day, the kid would get his mother a real big corsage from the tips he made, and they'd go out to dinner at a restaurant and take in a movie together. It was a real sweet sight to see, I used to be really touched. That kid would never, never let his mother work on Mother's Day. . . ."

Suddenly Angelo stood up, suffocating, choking on a strange anger. "What're you trying to prove?" he snarled. "You don't expect anybody to believe all that shit! You're out of your mind!"

"No, no, it's true, all of it," Sammy said soothingly. "Don't you like my stories?"

"It's all a lot of shit and I'll get as screwy as you if I keep sitting here and listening." His knees felt weak, and the cricket sound was amplified in his head.

"Don't get so excited, *bubi*," Sammy said, getting up and approaching him.

"I'm not excited. Forget it, forget it." Angelo tried to leave, but his legs would not move; the din of crickets gave way to a mounting sea-shell roar.

"I mean, it don't shock you, or anything like that, does it?" The pale face blurred as it came closer. "I mean, you're a tough little *luksh,* you're a scientist. You got this all figured out, don't you?"

"Look, I'm hot . . . tired. . . . The story hour is over for now. You're a great entertainer, but you don't shock me. Sorry to disappoint you. You don't do nothing. . . ."

"Yes, yes, sure." Sammy was so close now that he went completely out of focus.

The room began to spin. Angelo put his hands out for support. He heard voices as though from under water, ringings from far away. And then he was moving along the corridor, looking up at the ceiling. His cheek was against starched cloth that smelled of soap. Moving his gaze from the ceiling, he saw the long, dark nostrils, the great eyes, the light sea grass of hair.

He was being carried!

"What the hell are you doing? Goddam it, put me down." But weakness and amazement reduced the conviction in his voice. How easily Sammy carried him!

"It's all right, *boychik,* I'll let you rest on an empty bed for a while." There was a doorway; Sammy laid him on the drum-tight linens of a bed, and stood looking down with a sweet, mocking smile. "Heat prostration," he said. "Oh, sure, you get all excited when it's so hot and—boom—you *plotz.* And then, this place . . ." He looked around the room with an expression of amusement so remote that his smile was leafy and fragile. "All the statues of the rabbi around, and the kids crying, and the sick people . . . You could be looking at the whole world squinched down to a tiny reflection. And downstairs they're *kvetching* out the babies while up here . . . You see them all—weak, begging—it gives you a feel, like of . . . of power? I don't know, there's a lot of angles here. There's a lot of possibilities."

Angelo thought of going home and filling the tub with icy water and staying in it until everything leaped back into clear view. But for now he lay staring at the scattered parts of a jig-saw puzzle, confronted by random cuttings, half faces, arbitrarily curved fragments of color that made no sense in themselves. But he had to stop being angry—that just played into Sammy's hands.

"Thanks anyhow," Angelo said evenly. "Yeah, running around in that heat—I'll be okay."

Sammy didn't seem to be listening to him, but began to hum absently. The wail of an ambulance siren came from far off, grew louder intermittently, spiraled closer and closer.

"Don't you ever do any work, for Christ sake?" Angelo asked, staring at the window, which showed a deep, dirty brown in the faint glow of a streetlight. "How long you think you can keep a racket like this?"

"Oh, a long time yet, *bubi*. I did the same thing on a lot of other jobs before and I'll do it on a lot of jobs to come. Just don't worry your little *goyisha kop* about me."

"I'm not worried. Far as I'm concerned, they could can you tomorrow."

"But you don't mean that, do you, *bubi?*"

Angelo turned his head slowly and stared into Sammy's eyes. The siren reached fortissimo and then moaned away to silence. Angelo listened to the motor as the ambulance went down the ramp, brakes squealing. A door opened and closed. There were calm voices, and another door opened.

"No . . . no, I guess I don't," Angelo admitted in a thick, stunned voice. "And I want to know why the hell that's so."

"It's a mystery, hah?"

"There's a reason and I'll figure it out. I'll find out what you're up to. I know a few things, and I'll know more as time goes on."

Sammy laughed. "Maybe you wouldn't like what you found."

"I'm not worried. I never been afraid of facts."

"Ah, *facts*," Sammy said.

"Yeah, facts."

"Facts, facts, facts. O, facts, facts, facts . . ." He began a little soft-shoe dance on the polished squares of brown linoleum.

"I'm okay now. I'll be getting back to the store," Angelo said, without moving from the bed. "All I need is liquid; I'm probably dehydrated. If I get a good night's sleep . . ."

"Sure, *boychik* . . . Da, da, dum, dee dee . . . facts . . . da dee . . . that's all you . . . need." Sammy kept his eyes intently on his shuffling feet.

Angelo turned back to the dark window, angry at his own anger. He's mental, don't exaggerate him, he told himself.

There came a low rumble of thunder, too distant to mean rain. His body was completely without strength, and he wondered how long it would be before he could get up. The shuffling, pattering sound of Sammy's mad little dance came to him after a while with the far-off, breaking sound of the thunder, and Sammy's muttering accompaniment was like the narration of whatever obscure things were happening in the hot night.

He must have dozed briefly. When he opened his eyes, Sammy was gone and his body was drenched. He pushed himself away from the bed, picked up his carton, and went out into the corridor. No one was in sight.

From one of the rooms came a voice calling for Sammy. Angelo put his head through the doorway and asked the ashen-faced woman if she wanted a nurse.

"No, no," she said frantically, "not a *nurse*."

Angelo shrugged and went on.

Outside, he realized it might rain after all. A faintly cool wind explored his face, and the night cracked with great disintegrating noises. His insides writhed and he had a momentary impulse to run away from the city before something awful happened.

Then he mastered his panic and walked swiftly back to the store.

CHAPTER SEVEN

HE woke late the next day and immediately sensed the change in the weather. It was still hot, but the humidity had decreased dramatically, and although his head ached, he felt more like himself. Alone in the house, he dressed at leisure, although it was well past noon, wandering finally into the kitchen, where he found a note from his mother printed on a shirt cardboard.

WE WENT SHOPING. TAKE SOME EGGS.

While he waited over the eggs in the pan, he stared at the shedding wall, trying to understand the night before. Something in him had not stood up to strain. The facts . . . He grimaced. All right, there were flaws in him, weaknesses, needs. I mean, a person who travels alone all the time, he told himself, somebody like me who don't mingle, is bound to have some kind of neurotic crap come out sometimes.

His reading had taught him that the solitary incurs certain risks, and he knew that his own life was not ideal psychologically; he recognized that only total self-honesty kept him in balance. These past weeks he had made lazy excuses in order to avoid something difficult to understand; he had turned away, overwhelmed, from the enigma of Sammy's personality. But to make a beginning was fairly simple after all; either the orderly was completely insane, or else he was crazy in certain areas but abnormally shrewd in others. From that point he could begin to dissect. For one thing, there was something between Sammy and the patients. Now, where was he that time I almost seemed to catch him at something? he asked himself. Once in the emergency room and once in the corridor outside the hospital pharmacy. Medicines were kept in both places. Drugs! Yeah, yeah. And all those stories—they would act as a smoke screen. While one hand is busy demonstrating a complex movement, the other one performs the real manipulation. For the first time in weeks, Angelo felt equal to a stupid world.

Smoke rose from the burning eggs; he turned the gas off cheerfully and put the ruined breakfast into the sink. "Man don't live by eggs alone," he said, smacking the scabby wall with the flat of his fist, and shadowboxed his way to the icebox, helped himself to an orange, and stripped it with his teeth. He spat the peel into the rubbish bag, and then, sucking the orange, went out of the house with a book under his arm. He had the optimistic feeling that he might do quite well in his life.

"Good *afternoon*," Frank said as he entered the store. "Banker's hours, hey? I been busy as hell all morning. You really take advantage, Angelo. You take me for granted too much. Here I am trying to distill responsibility in you, training you. I want to make a good deal here for you and you go . . ."

"Why don't you do me a favor and fire me?" Angelo said, grinning.

"Is that a way to talk? You know how I feel about you. Dante was like a brother to me. *I* feel my obligations."

Angelo clucked mockingly.

"You're an awful cynical kid, you know that?"

"Ah, come on, why do we have to go through this routine? I'm a bargain for you, I don't owe you beans. Go on, will you, Frankie—go make some snake oil or something, hah?"

"You know, Angelo, you make me sad. There's not a ounce of affection in you, not a gram of human warmth. You fight everybody off all the time: me, the Church, your family, girls. . . ."

"Yeah, I have a tough time fighting off the girls," Angelo said.

"You're not that bad-looking. In fact my kid sister-in-law once said she thought you was kind of cute."

Angelo hooted incredulously.

"Your trouble is you don't like people. You're a . . . a . . ."

"Misanthropist," Angelo supplied.

Frank shook his head admiringly. "See, you're a smart kid, you read, you know—that's what makes it sadder." He squinted penetratingly at Angelo. "You know what I see in you?"

"No, Frank, I don't know what you see in me. Tell me, what do you see in me?"

"Go on, go on, mock me—it only makes me feel sorrier for you."

"You're a real Christian, Frankie."

"Okay, okay, but I'll tell you anyhow. I look at you and I see a very unhappy kid."

"Frank, let me tell you something. People are sad because they're stupid enough to keep expecting things that aren't coming to them. The thing with me is, I don't expect *nothing,* not one goddam thing!"

"I really got to laugh, how a young squirt like you acts like he knows more than me."

"If the shoe fits . . ." Angelo flipped a glass into the air and caught it behind his back, winking at Frank's startled gesture.

"All right, I can't talk to you. Go on, go to the hospital before I lose my patience," Frank growled.

Angelo's face and body seemed sucked inward, as though the outside pressure of air had become suddenly disproportionate to the pressure inside. He darted his head around toward the street, and Frank wondered at his own unconsicous power. What had he said to make Angelo's face so odd?

"What's going on over there?" Frank asked gently. "Is something bothering you over at the hospital?"

Angelo turned back as though he had forgotten Frank was there.

"What? Oh no, no, I guess not," he answered absently. He took his strip of paper from the cash register without looking.

"You sure you're all right, Ange?"

Angelo shrugged and walked off without answering.

Frank went to the doorway and stood looking at the short, wiry figure, and felt a profound pity that extended beyond Angelo to everyone—even, in a small way, to himself.

There was a room located on an inside corner of the first floor that was separated from others by an unoccupied chemistry lab. Angelo had just glimpsed Sammy's tall white figure going away from it, and now he stared at the patient, a pimply-faced boy near his own age, whose eyes had a glazed, sated look.

For a moment Angelo hesitated suspiciously. But then the quiet and solitude of that part of the building encouraged him. He walked boldly into the room and picked up the boy's arm.

"Whatta you want?" the boy asked thickly, almost indifferently.

"Just to know if you need anything from the store."

Angelo studied the dark red holes on the oniony flesh of the arm. There was one fresher-looking puncture, with a dew-drop of blood on it.

"Hey, whatta you doing?" the boy said, pushing up through the haze toward apprehension. "Leggo my arm. What the hell you doing? No, no, gowan, I don't want nothing from the store."

"Did that orderly give you a needle just now?"

"D'hell business is it of yours?"

"Just answer me or you'll be in a lot of trouble."

"Get the hell out of here before I call a nurse," the boy said, clumsy over the consonants.

"Go on, call the nurse, call the nuns too. I'll wait here while you do. We'll see what they think about them holes in your arm." He reached for the call button, which lay like a snake's head on the pillow. "Want me to do it for you?"

The boy darted his hand toward Angelo's arm, his fingers blunt and inaccurate. "No, no, wait. Okay, whatta you want?"

"I just want you to answer me. Tell me what I want and I won't tell nobody. I just got my own reasons."

"Okay, yeah, he give me a needle."

"Why?"

"Because I asked him to. I get a lot of pain and he's got

this stuff makes it go away." There was a mist of sweat over his lip and on his forehead; his eyes were shifty, with minute pupils.

"What's wrong with you?"

"Ulcerated colitis." The boy fixed his pinhole pupils on the ceiling.

"Did *he* come to *you* with the idea of the dope?"

"Yeah. He heard me yelling one night and he says he can fix me up. He did. Now he comes every day."

"Did you pay him for the stuff?"

"Yeah."

Angelo almost smiled. The air around him cleared and he felt huge and strong.

"And nobody noticed the holes in your arm, the nurses, your doctor?"

"Nah, who notices in a place like this? *They* give needles too. *Their* needles—shit! Nobody counts the holes. The doctor figures the nurse gave it, the nurse thinks the doctor. Chris' sake, I lay here yelling my guts out and all they say is, 'Behave yourself, act like a man. We're giving you medication. You got to be patient.' Shit, whatta they care? They're used to everybody yelling. They get bored. They give you a little this and a little that, and it don't help. This guy comes in and he talks to me. Then he slips that needle in and—boy! He's got a heart."

"But you pay him?"

"So what? Anyhow, I only had about twenty bucks, and he's been carrying me for nothing for over a week now."

"You mean he still comes, even though you don't pay him?"

"He don't even bother me about the dough no more." The boy turned his head on the pillow and closed his eyes. He looked dead and happy.

Walking down the corridor, Angelo recognized some lessening of his elation, but felt himself progressing generally. The reason he still gives the kid dope, even though he's out of dough, is so the kid don't have withdrawal fits. That would give the thing away. Besides, it don't cost him anything, the hospital got a huge supply. He decided, even though he needed no more confirmation, that he would examine the arms of other patients.

He went through the wards and the semiprivate and private rooms, and what he saw substantiated what he knew. But in the end the superfluity of evidence became a taunt that made his victory dry and empty. It had been too simple to figure out the orderly's game.

CHAPTER EIGHT

Nurses, nuns, doctors, all looked at him with an oddly harried expression when he arrived the next day to take the afternoon orders. There had been two policemen at the emergency entrance, and now, on the fifth floor, he watched a lieutenant talking to the head nurse. He walked past uneasily, conscious that another policeman, a sergeant, was examining him from head to foot.

He went over to the table where Sullivan was writing tiny numbers on a chart.

"What's going on, Sully?" he asked in an undertone.

"Well, it's pretty damned rotten. They ought to string people like that up!"

"What is it? I don't know what happened."

"Someone molested one of the kids." Her glance held him responsible in a small way.

He stared at her blankly.

"Someone tried to rape one of the kids over in the pavilion," she said in a low, murderous voice that had a certain angry pleasure in it. "For maybe ten minutes the sister stepped out and some guy got in there. The sister got back just in time and she didn't get to see him. They keep it so dark over there. He didn't actually get to—you know—do it, but the poor kid is in shock. It just gets you sick to think . . . If you could just have seen her. Her nightgown was torn and there was a . . . a real mess on the sheets. Echh, when I think . . ." She glared down at her chart, and Angelo became aware of the whispery atmosphere all around.

For a few minutes he stared sightlessly at her crisp white cap, perched like a great moth on the back of her head. Something seemed to crumble within him. What was this, what? His route opened onto a multitude of doors. The traffic of people was unusually dense and was darkened by the uniforms of the police. I should have just kept away from him. . . .

Sullivan muttered viciously. The halls were louder and more urgent with footfalls of uncushioned feet.

"Don't they . . . I mean, couldn't she say who . . . the kid . . ."

She looked up at him in exasperation. "She couldn't, she can't speak anyway. Besides, she's in shock. I told you."

"Oh, the kid with the thing in her throat?"

"I can't talk about it." She waved him away. "It just makes me sick."

"Do they suspect anybody?" he asked, perhaps only out of an obscure desire to protect himself.

"It has to be someone familiar with the hospital. They're questioning everybody."

Angelo looked around him, listening to the slightly altered sound of the place. The center of things had shifted from the rooms to the corridors, and there was a tendency on the part of all ambulatory people to gravitate toward others and begin talking; no one dared to stand alone.

While Angelo went about taking orders, he felt he was running the gantlet; in the elevator, a policeman who rode down with him stared at him unblinkingly the whole way; and on the first floor, despite the cluster of policemen and doctors who surrounded her, Sister Louise noticed his passing.

In that quiet corner of the floor where the pimply-faced boy was bedded, near the deserted lab, he walked more slowly, catching the breath he seemed to have lost.

"Angelo."

He turned spasmodically. Sammy stood spread-eagled against the wall, a mischievous agony on his face.

"They got me, *boychik*, I'm trapped like a rat. Oooh, it's getting dark, pal, I'm sinkin' fast. But before I go, pardner, I want you to promise you'll take care of Mary and the kids. You just got to promise me that, pal. I'll tell you where the loot is buried but . . ."

Angelo started to walk away.

"Hey, wait. Where you running?"

"You know what happened, God damn it," Angelo said in a harsh whisper. "I don't want anything to do with it."

"What happened? When?" Sammy asked innocently. "I mean, after all, there's always something happening. The Red Sea parted, a woman in Canada had five kids at once. . . ."

"With the kid!" It issued from him like live steam.

Sammy made an O with his mouth and nodded.

"Look," Angelo said, slumping in sudden exhaustion. "I know all about you. You're cooked goose, man."

"So who isn't cooked?" Sammy said mildly. "Life is a avalanche—the little stones only bruise you, the big ones kill you. What's the sense getting excited?"

A din of voices seemed to become slightly louder; footsteps threatened to come closer.

"Hey Sammy, don't bother with all that. I found out what you were doing with the drugs. See, you're no mystery to me. That was trouble enough, that was good enough reason for me to stay away from you. But this . . . Hey, I don't know, maybe you're sick. Either way, you had it. Either you better go talk to them, or else you better haul ass out of here—quick!"

"Talk to them? What talk? Words—they don't mean a thing. Nobody has any idea what they're saying anyhow. They're all numb, *bubi*, they're like radios, that's all."

"They questioned you?" He began toeing the floor nervously.

"Yeah, they questioned and questioned. I said, 'Ask no questions, I'll tell no lies.' I said, 'Go on, frisk me, boys, there's nothing up my sleeve, nothing in my head. Now observe, out of nowhere—*poof*—a fish dinner!'"

"You really don't realize, do you?" Angelo said, having trouble breathing as the voices and uncushioned footsteps drew casually closer. "Hey, you're in *trouble!*"

"All God's chillun got trouble."

"Don't it matter to you about the kid? Isn't any of this getting through your screwy brain? Do you even hear me talking?" He had an urge to shake Sammy, to drive his fist into the soft, pale features. The sounds were close, yet the two of them seemed to be held away from everything by a great glass pane.

"It's sad about the little girl," Sammy said calmly. "But there's other things too, worse things. . . ."

Just then a policeman came in sight at the turn of the corridor, and Angelo spun around and was off around the corner. He got outside, his ears ringing, his breath weighted so he could only inhale and exhale shallowly, and his run toward the store was really a falling forward.

"What do you mean, you didn't take any orders?" Frank shouted. "What the hell is the matter with you?"

"I couldn't. Something happened over there. The cops wouldn't let me go around," he said, panting, finding some relief in the lie.

"What cops? Who they think they are? What happened?"

"Someone tried to rape one of the kids in the pavilion."

"No!"

Angelo filled a glass with water, nodding.

"A *little* kid?" Frank said into his face.

"A little kid."

"Well, that's awful! Do they know who did it?"

But Angelo couldn't answer, even evasively: he was fascinated by a freakish accident to his vision; for some reason, he seemed to see everything through a long, slightly irregular frame, a frame shaped like the outlines of a face. No matter where he looked, his view was circumscribed by that disturbing limitation.

"Angelo, I'm talking to you! I said, do they know who did it?"

All Frank got for his effort was a shrug.

In the evening, Angelo went back under the command "Take orders or don't come back yourself." Frank was not the moving force however; Angelo was like a person in a cold country who knows that immobility is death. One way or another he would dig out his routes again.

He went first to the children's pavilion, where a policeman stood in bored attendance beside the night desk. Maria's bed was empty and he asked an old nun where and how she was.

"She's over in Main Private, poor creature," the nun said. "Her parents are with her now. Oh, I hope she'll be all right, but a thing like this can leave awful scars. Then, of course, her physical condition . . ."

"They pick up anyone yet?" he asked, merely making conversation.

"Yes, they arrested that Jewish fellow, and that Howard Miller."

"I always thought they were a little funny. A little off in the head."

"I don't know, it seems hard to believe that a man could do a thing like that."

Oh, the things about men that would surprise *you*, Sister, he thought, almost with pity—wandering around in a bestial world with only her little black book of fairy tales to lead her.

When he had taken the orders, gone back to the store and filled them, and finally delivered them, he found himself, as though by design, at the entrance to the fifth-floor solarium.

He went inside. In the corners the plants made an indecipherable meshwork of leaves and stems. The wheelchairs looked bereft; suddenly, without warning, he felt an onslaught of loneliness. Never before this moment had he been consciously unhappy about his solitude; now he glimpsed a massive crater in himself. But he had known all along that he was alone, he had accepted the fact of his accidental conception. Why now did he feel deprived?

He walked around the solarium, touching chairs, riffling

through the scattered magazines, whose pages might just as well have been blank for all he could see of them. The great building sighed and breathed like a restive creature; children cried thinly from across the cement yard, and the leaves of the beech tree whispered restlessly. Through the window he could see the new building under its roof light, seemingly arrested in construction, still without windows as it waited for some contractor to come in with the right price on the glass.

And suddenly an image of Sammy, obscenely exposed and tearing at the little girl's body, flashed like a light before him. Yet, despite the brevity of the vision, he had time to note the contradiction: in the midst of the act, the long, ugly face was still serene and gentle. He was startled by a moan. Then the room was dark again, and he was shaken by the realization that the sound had come from his own throat.

"Aw, come on now," he said aloud, with disgust. And then to himself: Now wait, *compa'*, you're emotional. Okay, face it. But he lacked the energy to draw upon the forces of reason; he just felt tired and depressed. He dragged himself down the corridor, with the carton trailing from his hand, and while he waited for the elevator, he thought more distantly about all of it. Guys like Sammy were twisted. Maybe the same things that he himself had had the psychological stamina to transcend had crushed reason in Sammy. There were reasons. . . .

His house was dark and sleeping, but he knew sleep would never come to him in his condition. A cold bath might have made a difference, but he didn't want to run the water for fear he would wake Dominic and his mother and then have to exchange words with them.

He stood uncertainly in the stuffy darkness, smelling that

eternal afterlife of food smell that haunts poor ho
odor that does not come from the stirring of good,
cooking but seems instead to be the pervasive curse of c
poverty. Around him, his family's breathing sounded in
ous rhythms: Dominic's phlegmy and scraping, his mother's
panting, Theresa's rather quick and shallow, each exhalation
ending with a tiny moan, as in the sleep of a young puppy.

He thought of the garden hose, and went out the back
door, unbuttoning his shirt as he walked. It was slightly cooler
here, or seemed so. He sat on the side porch steps, took off
his shoes and socks, slid off his pants, and then, with defiant
speed, stepped out of his undershorts.

Naked, he padded around, peering at the ground in search
of the hose until he stepped on it. Picking up the nozzle, he
followed the rubber length back to the faucet and turned it
on. There was a sputter and hiss, and he heard the water
raining on the leaves of the lilac bush near the fence. He
carried the hose end out into the center of the yard and
turned it toward him.

It struck his body with a wonderfully vivid chill. He blew
wetly at the water streaming over his face, rubbed the skin of
liquid that coated him, and seemed to breathe a marvelously
pure air through every pore. After a while he aimed the hose
straight up and stood, face to the sky, letting it rain on him.
A faint dripping came from the leaves of a nearby bush.

He squatted down and smelled the wet earth and the grass.
With surprise he felt a warmer flow on his cheeks, and real-
ized that he was crying. *But he had never expected anything!*
Why should he have this gnashing sensation of betrayal?

He didn't care what Sammy had done; the man was nothing to him. Nor were moral judgments in his line. Certain
things repelled him because he hated the untidiness of starved
passion, the stupidity of destruction.

Down on his haunches in the mud, he forced himself to view the act, detail by detail, to examine the motives and study the sources. More than anything, he aspired to that clinical and functional detachment that allows decent men who are doctors to exclaim with great professional delight over the discovery of a classic cancer growth, an attitude that was not callousness but single-minded dedication. He applied the sketchy knowledge he had obtained from his reading and dressed the visualized acts in technical jargon; with these words as rungs, he descended into the bowels of the crime. He was down there some time, bumping around under the low ceiling, straining to see into the myriad caves and passages with his feeble, flickering miner's lamp. And when he had seen as much as he could, with the appalling clarity he required, he found that he had discovered next to nothing.

He got up and padded to the steps, where he dried himself with his undershorts. Taking his clothing under his arm, he went into the house, and the denser air wrapped around him once more. He groped through the rooms, occasionally bumping into things and cursing softly because the furniture seemed to have been moved from the accustomed places.

Until he was in the doorway of the dining room and saw a figure silhouetted against the light from the street.

"Theresa?" he whispered.

"You're naked," his mother answered softly. "Don't you have any shame, to walk around like that?" Her voice was oddly lacking in anger; it sounded musing and strange instead.

"You don't have to look. I didn't think anybody would be up." He felt an unpleasant intimacy in their whispering and tried to cover himself with his clothes.

"I couldn't sleep," she said in a faint, wailing voice. Her breasts and belly were outlined by the pale light, hardly obscured by the thin nightgown. "Lots of nights I can't sleep.

When it's hot like this I get feeling funny. My body gets restless. Like I want something and I can't think what. I get up for a drink of water, take something to eat. It don't help. I don't know. . . . Oh, I'm a young woman yet—I think of your father in such a way. . . . I was in the kitchen before and I saw you in the yard. You looked like him, all flat and hard. . . . Oh my God, I'm a sinful woman. But I can't sleep, Angelo, I can't sleep. . . ."

"Shut up, do you hear me! I don't want to hear your sick dreams. You're a hypocrite. Even now you're pretending. One minute you're telling me it's a shame to walk around naked, and the next breath you're saying how you're starved for a man. And even that you won't say right out. You and your brother, is that what I'm supposed to use for an example?" He panted with a rage and disgust that poured out of him like blood. "You better go to bed before Dominic wakes up," he snarled. "Go kiss your cross, go sleep with that!"

"I didn't know you hated me, Angelo. Am I that bad a mother?" She was like an unknown woman. The dimness gave her a horrifying beauty; the outline of light allowed her stature enough for tragedy. And yet he knew that, at best, she deserved only pity. "Don't you see," she said. "I'm fed by crying, I wear black. But I feel like wearing a red dress and singing songs. I'm not dead, I'm *not!*"

She began to weep, and Angelo stood there, as bare as when he had come from her body, paralyzed with anger and fear, unable for the moment to summon the understanding that would make their separation bearable.

"How can you run to the church every day? How can you cross yourself with every other breath?"

"I *want* to believe, I *try*. I live like a nun, but I'm not a nun. How could I keep from going crazy if I didn't hope for something from heaven? Is this a life for a person otherwise?"

"*I* don't need spooks to live. You make the ghosts and

then you bawl because you're afraid of them. Don't come to me. I don't hate you, but there's nothing between us, not a goddamned thing! All around me I see people making fancy filth. Why can't they be clean and honest? Why can't you? I believe that what goes up has to come down unless you get out past the earth's gravity. I believe that there's only lies and truth—if you want the lies, then have them."

"Is it so simple?" she whispered bitterly. "Don't you know how much goes on in the dark?"

"You *make* the dark, you *want* it!"

"It's *there*," she wailed.

"It's there if you keep your eyes closed."

"Oh, you're so hard, so cold. I can't believe you came from my own body."

"That was something you didn't want to remember, either."

"But you, don't *you* have a feeling for your mother?"

"That part's nothing. Flowers have their pollen blown around in the wind; the seeds don't celebrate Mother's Day."

"You make me feel like killing myself."

"Don't do that. You'd only have your body thrown into a unconsecrated grave," he said flatly. "Get yourself a man instead."

She began to sob quietly, her face in her hands. Angelo left her and went into his own room. His bed was warm and dry and he lay on it, feeling as porous and lifeless as a cinder. He heard his mother's soft crying gradually diminish into a series of sighs.

Finally he fell asleep, and he dreamed terrible, erotic dreams that involved him and his mother and Theresa and Sammy and the girl with the tube in her throat. When he woke, very early in the morning, he got up and washed the semen from his body with a weary, preoccupied air, wondering what he was going to do.

CHAPTER NINE

THE police came that night, while Angelo was eating supper. With an obsequious expression Dominic led them into the living room, and returned to the kitchen for Angelo.

"Cops," he said accusingly to Esther. "There's your son for you. Go on, they're in the living room, go ahead."

Esther stared wildly at her son. "What is it, what'd you do?" she cried, her waxy face flushed; it was as though she anticipated Angelo's persecution for something she herself had done. Angelo said nothing; he just got up and went to the living room, where he sprawled on the couch, as comfortably as if the two uniformed men hadn't been there at all. The one with the sergeant's stripes pulled a chair roughly under him, so that his knees almost touched Angelo's. Dominic, in the doorway, watched uncertainly; Esther peered over his shoulder, her hand covering her mouth to keep her fear from bursting out. In the formality of the policemen's blue-black uniforms and brass buttons, her house seemed ready to tumble down, and her fear was mixed with shame.

"Your name is Angelo DeMarco?" the sergeant asked, pen to pad.

"A, as in angel, N, as in nothing . . ."

"I can spell it. Your age?"

"Nineteen."

"How long you lived here?"

"All my life," Angelo said to the farthest corner of the room.

"Ever been in any trouble?"

"All my life," he repeated monotonously. He had the unpleasant feeling that someone was drawing stitches from a wound on his body; a wave of dismay made him curl his mouth and look scornfully into the policeman's eyes.

The sergeant lowered his pad and leaned closer, with a threatening expression. "Look, sonny, if you're gonna be a wise guy, you're only gonna make it tough on yourself. We're not playing games. Now, I don't know if your family understands what this is all about . . ." He turned to Dominic, charging him with the keeping of order.

"I don't know *nothing*, lieutenant," Dominic said.

"Sergeant," he corrected.

"We're law-abiding people. I could get a personal recommendation from Captain Battapaglia down in precinct. He's in the K. of C. with my sister's cousin by marriage. He'll tell you . . ."

"A little girl over at Sacred Heart was sexually molested," the sergeant interrupted.

Dominic turned black. For half a minute he stood in silence; then he sputtered with almost sincere indignation, "If *he* had anything to do with it . . ."

"Nobody said he did. We think we got the guy responsible, but we still have to square everything up. We have to question anybody familiar with the hospital."

Dominic subsided.

"All right now, sonny, if we're all straightened out about things. Let's have some civil answers, huh? *Have* you ever been in trouble—with the police?"

"No," Angelo answered.

"What kind of fellas you pal around with, Angelo?"

"I don't pal around with anybody."

The sergeant studied him, and wrote something down, perhaps just an unofficial note to himself. "I suppose you go out with girls."

"You suppose wrong." Angelo's face betrayed his scorn for such tactics.

The sergeant studied him at length now, covering his own uncertainty with a professional glare. "How well did you know this Jewish guy and this fairy, Miller?" he finally asked.

"I don't know—pretty well."

"You spend much time with them?" the sergeant asked, gaining confidence.

"We used to sit in the solarium at the hospital and talk."

"Talk about what?"

"I don't know." Angelo's eyes clouded with a perplexity so genuine that the sergeant's anger diminished. "I couldn't tell you."

The sergeant stood up. "Okay, sonny, that's all for now. Just stick around where we can find you if we need you. We might want to talk to you again." He tucked his notebook into his pocket, nodded at his assistant, and went to the door, ignoring Dominic's solicitous escort. But he stopped for a moment and looked back through the house with a frown before he followed his assistant out, slamming the door behind him.

The crash focused Dominic's anger. "So," he said. "That's the kind of filth you get mixed up in, hah?"

"I'm not mixed up in anything."

"Yeah, you been building up to something rotten all your life!"

"Why you trying to start something now?" Angelo asked wearily.

"*I'm* not starting anything, don't go blaming *me*. I'm just getting sick and tired of being the brute around here. You get mixed up in shit and *I* smell, hah?"

"Look, let's just drop it."

"You walk around here like we're all shit to you!" Dominic cried, as though at last his anger had found an opening through which to spill. "You laugh at Jesus Christ hisself!" A thousand bitter things found sudden egress. Pulled up by the roots, his frustration forgot that it had come from an old seed of love. His nephew's face was a warped, scored version of a five-year-old face he had once been able to kiss. Neither Esther nor Theresa had ever confused or deluded him, but Angelo had betrayed him to his own soft heart. "Well, I'm fed up, you hear? If you can't start acting like a human being, I don't want you here in my house. You're not special, you're a little dago snot who thinks he's better than everybody else. I don't want no more of your disrespect of God or the Church or me!" His voice trembled with the pleasure of release; a vein stood out beside his black-pocketed eyes. "The priest comes to me and asks how come you live outside the Church. I don't know what to say, I'm embarrassed—he thinks I'm

94

responsible. Then the cops come into my house, and I'll have to explain that to people. I don't want no more!"

"Leave me alone, Dominic." Angelo's flat, matter-of-fact voice was an affront; he knew it, and didn't care. If he remembered ancient moments of warmth against his uncle's cigar-and-wine-smelling face, he felt no more obligation to them than he did to his mother's physical pain at his birth.

"*Uncle* Dominic, goddam you!"

Angelo got up and started for the door.

"Bastard!" Dominic shouted. He pulled Angelo's shoulder, spinning him around, and slapped him—forehand, backhand, and forehand, in rapid succession. But then he was appalled by the force of his nephew's leap backward. Angelo, crouched and taut behind his face, expressed pure murder.

"Touch me again, I'll kill you," he gasped, fitting the words between his teeth.

Esther stood weeping a room away.

"Get out of my house, you Sicilian bastard," Dominic cried, his dark eyes leaking tears of fury and anguish. "Get out, get out, get out."

Angelo went into the bedroom and stacked up his clothes; they made a small pile. Brushing past his weeping mother, he entered the kitchen and found two large paper bags. Esther followed him back into the bedroom and spoke his name in lugubrious appeal, but he paid no attention to her.

When the bags were full, he looked around to see if there was anything else he should take with him. He had packed his few clothes and one or two of the books; the rest he could pick up some other time. It briefly occurred to him that there should be something momentous about this; he was leaving the house in which he had spent almost all of his life. *Was* there something for which he could feel regret? Hadn't there perhaps been certain moments of joy or even sweet-ness? He had slept here, dreamed here, wakened on thousands of mornings to enter into thousands of days from this room and this house.

He looked at the tumultuous pattern of the wallpaper, the mass-produced crucifix, the shabby, ugly furniture. His uncle was still ranting and cursing in the living room. Angelo shrugged and smiled grimly; he blew a kiss at the air. Then he picked up his paper-bag luggage and walked to the front door.

"*Angelo,*" his mother wailed, her hands stretched out, but she really didn't know what she wanted from him.

For a moment he paused in the doorway, wondering where Theresa was just then. Finally he went out of the house and down the street, as strong as Lot any day of the week.

At first, Frank took the news with uncharacteristic silence. But in the evening, after Angelo's final trip to the hospital, he could no longer resist sermonizing and turned to his cousin with a look of doleful affection.

"And where'd you sleep last night?" he asked, his doggy face so sadly sweet it seemed about to dissolve.

"I didn't sleep. I sat in the Waldorf cafeteria and drank coffee. I had a book to read."

"You coulda called me." Frank's face wrinkled in exquisite pain. "I coulda put you up for the night."

"What's the difference?"

"Angelo, Angelo, you're ruining your life."

"Never mind, *compa'*. There's nothing much to ruin."

"What're you gonna be—a sour old hermit living in fur-nished rooms all your life? You'll end up one of these char-acters the kids laugh at, sitting on the green with your books, mumbling in your beard. Loosen up, you're just a kid yet.

Make friends, learn a trade—*something*. Hey, I had just as tough a childhood, and look at me."

"Okay, Frank, that's all right," Angelo said consolingly. He picked up his two paper bags, ready to leave.

Frank winced at that poor luggage and banished Angelo with a wave of his hand even before he had left the store.

The woman at the boardinghouse showed him into a tiny back bedroom that looked out upon a quiet, narrow yard, all overgrown with bushes.

"Linens once a week," she said cautiously, looking for objections. She had a broad, lavender face and tight, wiglike white hair; Angelo knew her from the store as a regular muscatel customer. "I keep a quiet place here. Don't smoke in bed, and no food in the room—it brings ants."

When she left him, he took his things out of the bags, spreading his clothing thin enough to occupy two of the drawers in the bird's-eye maple bureau, whose swollen front was losing its veneer. His books he stood on top, beside his brush, toothpaste, and toothbrush.

Then he looked around with a rather abashed feeling of modest pleasure. Well, it was his own room and he didn't have to share it with anyone; for the first time in his life he would sleep in a room by himself. One may live in a grim place, but a slight breeze of pleasure can momentarily bring release. He smiled.

First he sat on the bed, bouncing a few times, with his hands out on the faded Indian blanket. Next he got up and went to the window, almost imagining a different sky would be visible from there. After a while he sat in the black carved armchair whose upholstered seat leaked stuffing; there was a small mirror on the door, and in it he caught a glimpse of his foolish smile.

Finally he undressed, switched off the light, and lay on the bed with a feeling of excitement he thought would keep him awake. In no time he was sleeping.

He dreamed of a summer evening in the southern town in which they had lived briefly while his father was alive, a place he seemed to remember only through his mother's rare mention of it. Yet as he played in the warm dusk it was all so familiar to him that he knew each fence, each rooftop. There was a smell of vanilla and lilac so intense that it seemed he must wake and find it really existed; all around him was a joy as towering as an immense tree. Suddenly he heard his name called, and he walked toward a lighted doorway. A tall, beautiful man with a mustache smiled and beckoned to him. He began to run, to run toward . . .

Then it was icy cold and he was standing on a hill like a slag heap. He was part of a circle of many people, each of whom held a sharp stone in his hand and scraped at the flesh of his neighbor—without anger, solemnly, with an air of preoccupation. A woman bent toward him, jabbing at his hands, which were bloody but still capable of holding his own sharp stone. He slashed her bare breasts, and a perplexity floated to the surface of his anguish; he couldn't tell which caused him the most pain—what she did to him or what he was doing to her. All around was the low, painful moaning; the world was in a gun-metal light and cold beyond hope. The woman smiled horribly and said, "Yes, *boychik,* yes . . ." He cried out in terror.

Someone knocked at the door. He opened his eyes and stared at the mirror, which cast back a faint light from outdoors.

"What is it?" the landlady whispered loudly.

"It's all right," he answered. "I was dreaming." But he wasn't sure that this exchange wasn't part of the dream.

She cleared her throat and mumbled uncertainly, "Well, all right, then. . . ."

After that he dozed off and slept dreamlessly until morning. When he got up and dressed, he still enjoyed the unaccustomed privacy, but last night's elation was gone. For a while he stood at the window, staring out at a yard that, revealed by daylight, looked as shabby as Dominic's. The neighborhood was quieter; the buildings he could see were old red-brick nurses' homes and internes' quarters, the back of a restaurant. There were untended grapevines, a few ailanthus trees, a rusty trash burner, and a clothesline from which hung a white sheet torn in three places.

As he stood there something snaked up into his consciousness, and the whole reason for his being in this room spread anguish through him.

CHAPTER TEN

THAT evening, Angelo's last delivery was to McKenna, the red-haired technician who worked in the autopsy room and who also attended to the hospital pharmacy.

"How's business?" Angelo asked, handing him the carton of soda.

"In here . . ." McKenna shrugged, and began blithely sipping through the straws.

The stench of formaldehyde almost made Angelo gag; he tried to keep his eyes away from the corpse lying on the drainer. But then, fascinated by McKenna's remarkable composure, he forced himself to look at it.

"Cirrhosis," McKenna said politely, following his gaze.

"None of this stuff bothers you, does it?" Angelo studied the colorless, dead flesh of what had been a middle-aged man.

"It's a job. Besides, the stiffs are no trouble. It's quiet down here, orderly, neat. I'll take it any day over upstairs; I can't stand to see people in pain."

"You're very sensitive." Now Angelo found he could look at the body without too much effort.

"Yeah, inside I'm all mush," McKenna admitted sadly, tucking the dead arm a little closer to the torso with the absent gesture of a housewife flicking at a grain of dust.

What *was* all the fuss, Angelo wondered. Perhaps if he had had McKenna's job he would have been invulnerable to the confusion of the past several weeks. People should be considered in the way that the florist thinks of flowers, as things that are grown just to be cut, ultimately to wither and die. No incantations, no spooks; just the laws of pollenization, of blown seed in a random wind.

"Nah, this place is fine," McKenna said. "It's that goddam drug room gives me the headache. I mean I never *could* make the inventories tally, but *lately* . . . Jeez, it's like the place sprung a leak. Anytime now I'm gonna have the superintendent or Sister Louise down on me. I'm afraid for my job. I'll take the stiffs *any*time."

"I hope you don't lose your job, McKenna," Angelo said, beginning a thought he could not quite recognize yet.

"Well, if I don't figure out them drugs . . ."

"Okay, McKenna." Angelo went to the door of the basement room.

"You gotta run right off? It's okay down here, but sometimes it's nice to have someone to talk to. I get a little afraid for myself, talking to them." He waved at the body.

"I'll catch you tomorrow." Angelo moved out into the dim, underground corridor.

The air was close and dusty. Overhead, great swollen steam pipes wove around each other and stretched into the murky recesses where there were no lights. Half the bulbs were gone, but in the near-dark Angelo could make out the gleaming shapes of oxygen compressors and spare beds. Here and there were other pieces of equipment: lamps, elaborate folding stretchers, diathermy machines, peculiar racks and carts. The corridor had the look of an old dungeon strewn with elaborate instruments of torture, things that made people live in pain for a longer time than was good for them.

The smell of ether was oddly strong down there, too; all the medicinal scent of the hospital might have emanated from this shadowy cellar.

He clanked against pails, brushed against dangling rubber tubing and spiderwebs. There was a huge, low humming from the ventilation system. Vague creakings and scurryings just touched his hearing. Now and then a clicking came from the elevator motor somewhere in the dark as the machinery selected floors.

Someone stepped out of an alcove, and he caught his breath as though it were the last one. A figure clad in white . . . But low, massive . . .

"What do you . . ." He recognized Lebedov.

"Please, please," Lebedov rasped. "I got to talk to you. Can't sleep no more. Is hurt so Jeez Chris' awful I can't tell you!"

Angelo pressed back against the wall, his heart trying to wear itself out. As the broad, powerful figure closed on him he was filled with terror, because, even though he knew it was Lebedov, he couldn't make out the man's face. A short distance away McKenna would be moving peacefully around in his dissecting room. The ventilation system hummed mercilessly. He had the feeling he was trapped by a mindless force, and his terror was pure and uncomplicated for a moment. Until he gasped, "What do you want?"

And Lebedov answered, "I *want*," in a shredded, wailing voice of human agony.

Angelo slid along the wall, one hand behind him, feeling the feltlike texture of the calcimined cement. He needed desperately to find more room for himself, as though he and Lebedov filled to bursting the underground corridor. When an intersecting wall stopped him, he stood still and waited for the unguessable attack.

"Doan yell," Lebedov beseeched, his hands held out as though there were a net between them. His breath was as rank as a dog's. "I just got to tell you."

Angelo slumped helplessly against the soft wall. Yet in the black misery of the place he felt a queer sensation of belonging; a neglected part of him opened to a resignation that was almost like peace. The elevator motor was quite near and clicked with a grotesquely tranquil sound. His breathing fell into and then out of cadence with Lebedov's, and he stared through the darkness at the hunched mass of the old man.

"Lemme tell you, listen," Lebedov said, standing still and blocking Angelo in. "People is animal. What they are! I come from Russia. See my father drunk all time like crazy. Why? From being poor? From being scare? Maybe from being out in the sun, under sky like ant? Maybe from God, or from no God? Maybe from being hungry, from being alone in his head? Like a animal, but only worse, because something make him think he's not no animal? But what? My father . . . He come home in the night, burn like fire. I feel him hot from outside already. I hear him bark like he's a wolf with hot stones up his ass, hear him scream and sing and howl at the sky. Mother, she close her eyes without cry. We all stop breathe. He come in twenty feet tall. He walk to Mother and pull back her head by her hair and look in her face with eyes all blood, and mouth open like to eat her. And he scream, 'You ugly, you so ugly! What I'm gonna do with you?' And then when she stay with her eyes closed like dead, he punch her face and her body, and when she fall down he kick her all over. And he crying himself, like he's begging her for something. Then one night landlord kick him in pants all the way down village street, in front of everybody. Then Father get terrible drunk again. He come in that night, whispering, 'No more man any more, no more man, I'm free, free. . . .' His eyes was so wild, like he can't see nothing. I don't remember, all mix up. . . .

"He try to fuck my sister. Everybody screaming. Candle get knock over. Is dark like the bottom of the ocean and we all rolling around together there. Finally candle get light again. I don't know who made it—me, Mother, I don't know. And Father is laying on the floor with Mother standing over him. Is knife in her hand and Father bleeding all over his chest. I try not to see. She put him in bed and wash him around. He don't look at her, just up at ceiling. Sister on other bed, all curl up, dress tore. Mother sit by him, rock back and forth. Finally he dies.

"People kill like anything. Nobody give a shit. What is there? I go in church when I'm a boy. I like the pretty color windows, clothes on priest, nice funny smell. I pray Jesus Chris' in white robe with hands on head of kids. So, so . . . don't make no goddam difference. *People!* Just only they drink, eat, grab things, take womans.

"One time I read book man gives me, later read another. Tells me how Church no good, we should make revolts on Church, change things. Okay, *bam, bam,* smash him, right? Get food for poor peoples, make it so poor peoples don't have to bow down in front of rich big shots. Okay, fine?

Aghh, whatta you talkin'—only same damn thing all over again. Still everybody smash one each other, same crazy stuff!

"I get tired of that. It's no sense. So I just grab things my own self. What you want—take. Like I see pretty butterfly. Okay, I sneak up, grab him to enjoy. But he's such a little thing, he get all crush in my hands, all smash up with dusty feel on my fingers. And all everything the same, same way. I get old, it's worse. Nothing taste good no more, nothing smell good no more. Womans all dry up, fuck like old bone. Whole thing, aghhh . . ."

Gradually Lebedov's voice had gone higher and frailer; it began to take on a monotonous, rhythmically wailing quality, like a litany. Angelo, nodding without volition, felt a rawness inside; he wondered how all of this had aimed itself at him. It occurred to him that Sammy's crime might be even greater than he had imagined.

"Now is black all over," Lebedov went on. "Hurt like from knife. Wife suffocate me in my bed, cannot breathe. I'm not understand, dizzy all the time, dizzy. . . . That Jew talks, he makes my head go round and round and round. . . . I don't know . . . one time he make me sad like to die, next minute so happy I can't stand it.

"Crush little butterfly, you know? Try and grab him, is so pretty, so beautiful. Makes pain in my heart. *What is it?* Oh yeah, just eat, sleep—sure. But sometimes want little pretty . . . something. Is crazy? Like I am boy, I am with Father in meadow. I see butterfly. Father say, 'Hey, Dmitri, want butterfly?' I say to him, 'Yes, yes, please!' Father laugh. He grab butterfly, *tight.* Then he give it to me—how? I tell you how—all crush, like paste. No good like this, not pretty like this. I vomit and vomit and he laugh.

"See, I grab pretty thing, I want so bad I not care for nothing. But gets all squash. Aghh, what I should *do?* What for I need that crazy guy? Why he's not leave me alone, leave me get old, leave me die, leave me forget whole goddam thing? Pretty things . . . what, not real? Just is dream? Grab pretty little thing—get all lousy ugly. Is animal? So then why I hurt like this? Oh, Mother God . . . Hail Mary, full of grace . . . Oh, oh, oh, oh, Jesus Chris', Jesus Chris' . . ."

And then the old man's terrible weeping began to rage through the dark corridor. It burst the walls and went rampaging through the building, past the plaster statues and the floating figures of the nuns, past the doorways that framed a hundred varied agonies, each detailed by rubber tubes or metal machinery or rumpled linens, and finally out to the open street, where all the cries were muffled and lost in the immensity of the night-time sky.

A slant of light came from down the corridor and McKenna's head was revealed in the open doorway, squinting and perplexed as he looked for the source of the noise, irritated briefly by the pandemonium of the living after hours of immersion in his peaceful morgue.

Angelo, knowing now that there was nothing here to fear, that there hadn't been all along, fought up through the unaccustomed pity that had formed in the strangeness and just listened carefully, as though he had a plan to record all of it for some future study. Lebedov's crying seemed to fill the whole world.

"What's going on?" McKenna said, squinting his way toward them behind a lighted match; his voice brought everything back to scale, and Lebedov became, once more, a dirty old man crying fearfully in a discovered hiding place. "They ought to put some bulbs down here once in a while." McKenna lit another match and gaped at the old man.

"*You* did it, didn't you, Lebedov?" Angelo said tonelessly. "*You* tried to screw that kid."

106

Lebedov rocked back and forth, grasping his face, trying to crush it between his hairy, brutal fingers. His moans came low and shapeless from his throat. Watching his kneading, squeezing fingers, Angelo thought: That's a hard way to kill yourself—by the face.

"What is it, what's going on?" McKenna shouted, turning from one to the other of them.

Angelo just thumbed wordlessly at Lebedov, struggling to find his voice. "He's the one," he said at last, breathing heavily.

McKenna stood there scratching his head. The match burned his finger; he cursed, and lit another. "What?"

"The kid—he's the one tried to screw the kid."

McKenna turned slowly to study Lebedov, his mouth pursed to a silent whistle. McKenna spent his days in a morgue, his nights in a furnished room with the sound of drunken paupers for his lullaby. All his life had been passed at the level from which there rarely seems any danger of an injurious fall, so he had no tendency toward righteousness. There was only surprise and a bemused, habitual pity in his eyes. "Oh boy!" he said respectfully. "Ho-*leee!*"

The two of them looked at Lebedov, and to Angelo, the old man seemed to have changed imperceptibly in being revealed to another person.

From somewhere, the ringing of a telephone penetrated faintly into the dark basement; the sound emphasized the enormous weight of the building—all the immensity of weight that hung over them, that could crush them. They could have been trapped miners, measuring their breaths, waiting for the air to give out.

Finally Angelo pushed lightly at Lebedov's arm and jerked his head toward the lighted doorway. Lebedov looked at him and he nodded. Then the three of them walked to the dissecting room, squinting at its fluorescent brilliance.

Lebedov dropped into a chair, moaning, his hands again covering his weeping face, and McKenna looked at Angelo questioningly from where he stood behind the corpse.

"Call upstairs," Angelo said. "Tell them what it's all about."

He sat down opposite Lebedov and watched him; he felt inhumanly calm and for a few minutes couldn't imagine anything ever bothering him again. Behind him McKenna made his call in a quiet voice, and turned back to watch Lebedov as silently as Angelo.

After a while, Lebedov stopped moaning and lowered his hands; but he kept rocking back and forth in the chair, his eyes frosted by some great exertion, like birth. He rocked with expressionless pain, moving and moving but getting nowhere, his hands slack, his eyes already a great distance into hell.

Don't take it so hard, Lebedov, Angelo said to himself. It's not as bad as all that. After you're dead you're as well off as a saint. So you were hungry, but when you reached you got your hands slapped. It happens all the time, pop. Hey, Lebedov, how can *you* worry about hell?

The elevator mechanism kept switching discreetly; the ventilators hummed. There were no windows to tell them about the light outside. Deep under the earth they waited, and Angelo imagined a hell just like this: a place with soft, regular, metallic noises, three men and a corpse, endless waiting.

But the waiting did end. Two policemen pushed in aggressively; they were there for a half minute before they switched off their flashlights.

"Okay now," said the policeman with the ax-shaped head. "Who called? What's this all about now?"

"Hey, Civitello, it's me, McKenna."

"Oh yeah, whatta you say, McKenna?" The face relaxed

slightly. "What's going on? I couldn't figure out from the phone. You didn't . . ."

"The old man here," McKenna said, looking uncomfortably at Lebedov, who now sat red-eyed and stoical; he felt an impropriety in speaking about Lebedov in his presence.

"Come on, McKenna, what's going on?" the short fat policeman said; he was only a supernumerary, retired from active duty by age and so inclined to postures of vigor. "We're very busy. . . ."

"Well, it seems like he was trying to say . . ."

Angelo cut him off harshly. "He's the one who tried to rape the little girl. He's the one, so you better take him."

"Now, wait a minute," the ax-headed officer said. "Are you trying to say . . ."

"I'm telling you that he's the guy who tried to fuck that kid," Angelo said furiously. "Do you want me to draw a picture? Ask him, for Christ sake!"

Civitello, who had never encountered anything worse than a drunk before, looked around for some superior to make a decision. "Well now, wait a minute, hold on here. . . . Is this true, pop, is he telling the truth?"

Lebedov began rolling his head around very slowly. The policemen stared incredulously at him, fingering their night sticks and shuffling their feet. Finally Lebedov closed his eyes as though in some kind of assent, and Civitello, after looking briefly at his fat colleague, walked over to Lebedov. "Okay then, pop, let's see what this is all about, huh? Come with me and come quiet, okay?"

Lebedov startled him by standing up and walking to the door. The policemen followed, hastily, perhaps thinking he planned escape; but Lebedov stopped in the doorway and looked back at Angelo. His eyes were an atrocity; they could have belonged to a tiger who acquires, in the midst of feeding on the flesh of a man he has just killed, the curse of human understanding. Angelo had to look away from him; he fixed his gaze upon McKenna's immaculate linoleum floor.

"Boy," McKenna finally said. "How do you like that? Old Lebedov—Jee-zuss! You just can't figure. I mean, he's gotta be mental, wouldn't you say?"

"Sure, sure he is." Angelo lifted his gaze to the corpse. "All these characters . . . Of course, what else?"

"I mean, to try a thing like that on a little kid . . ." McKenna shook his head; perplexed to surfeit by the living, he looked tenderly at his corpse.

"Guy's got to be nuts," Angelo said emphatically.

"No other explanation."

"Some kind of brain damage. The brain is a funny thing—just take one lobe and put a little pressure on it . . ."

"Hey, you said it—absolutely!"

"You can be born with it," Angelo insisted. "Get it from the genes, or a mutation. You must of seen some of the pictures of what the Bomb done to babies?"

"Awful! That brain damage! Like a cousin of mine who had a kid with no arm. And a guy I went to school with, his brother was twenty-five years old and had a mind like a baby—they even used to keep him in a crib. Had no control—shit, piss, the works, didn't know up from down. He even looked like a wrinkled little old baby, if you can picture a wrinkled little old baby. I mean, I could never get it through my head that he was twenty-five years old, but this kid says, yeah, he's twenty-five years old, but I just . . ."

"What're you bullshittin', McKenna!" Angelo snarled suddenly. "Stop bending my goddam ear!"

McKenna stood transfixed, staring at Angelo's face. Finally he nodded. "Okay, sure, Angelo. How about a slug of soda,

110

hah? My mouth got dry from all that. I got some in the fridge. Come on, Angelo, how 'bout it?"

"No, no, I don't want nothing," Angelo answered in a dead voice.

He felt strangely old and tired, and he looked up at Mc-Kenna's red, friendly face. "Hey, I guess they'll let Sammy go. I guess they'll *have* to do that now."

For some reason the thought made him feel much worse.

CHAPTER ELEVEN

A DAY passed. Angelo went about his work in a torpor pierced only by a sudden preoccupation with the small details of his physical poverty. His shoes were cracked, his pants worn thin as a dustcloth. Clean though his shirt was, a stain of spilled chocolate that had survived many washings haunted its front, and there was a soft-edged hole in the breast pocket. For the first time he *felt* shabby and ugly, and he became profoundly unhappy about his appearance.

Now he noticed people in good clothes, people with fine large bodies and handsome faces. A blackness descended on him; it shocked him to realize how little he had ever had. Why had he not aimed for things within reach? The scientist! That was too funny for laughter.

When he returned to the store in the dark, to fill the evening orders, he blurted out his resentment.

"Frank, I want a raise."

"What're you talking about? Stop crapping around and fill the syrup pumps."

"I'm serious, Frank." He stood demandingly at the counter; the overhead light on his face ruled out levity.

"All of a sudden? What's the idea in the middle of the night?"

Angelo's silence was formidable.

"Look, we'll talk it over tomorrow, hah? Meanwhile, fill the orders, take care of the syrup pumps. . . ." Frank tried to get back to what he had been doing, but couldn't remember what it was. He grimaced; Angelo's demand had given him heartburn. "Falls in like an explosion," he muttered. "Like it's a goddam emergency."

"It is a goddam emergency. You pay me thirty-five bucks a week for eighty-five hours' work. I want ten bucks more right away." His voice alarmed Frank because it didn't seem to care one way or the other.

"Right away? This minute? What, have you got a gun? Are the bookies after you? I tell you what—why don't you just hit me over the head and tap the till yourself? Jeez, like a nut! Ten dollars right away. Honest to God, Angelo, you gotta learn restraint."

"I want an answer now," Angelo said coldly.

"Now, wait a minute." Frank's face was flushed. "First off, I believe in merit raises. You haven't got more valuable to me lately. In fact, you been worse these last few weeks. Now that you're bringing it up, I got a few gripes too. For one thing, you been absent-minded, you make mistakes with change. Then, I don't know *what* you been doing over at the hospital. You go over there at night and you're gone for hours. Don't forget—time is money. And the last few days the orders look like you only went to a half a dozen rooms. I don't see where you got any special claim to a raise now."

"Then I'll quit. There sure as hell isn't any point to this job anyhow."

"What got into you all of a sudden?" Frank exploded, shaken out of smugness by the thought of Angelo's leaving him. "Let's talk it over instead of going off half-cocked. I mean, even the goddam unions talk things over."

Angelo sat on one of the counter stools and began tracing the veins in the marble with his finger. "I just realized. Yeah, I just realized that I don't have a friggen thing. Now, don't tell me I'm feeling sorry for myself—not that I care what you say anyhow. The truth is, that's not it. To feel sorry for yourself you got to feel that somehow you been taken, that you're not getting what's coming to you. I don't think anything is coming to anybody. If you're dumb enough not to take, then you don't get. And just suddenly, today, I decided I want something that it's possible for me to have. I started figuring and, my God . . ." He gave a little iron chuckle of amazement. "You know, Frank . . ." He looked up from the counter. "I got as little as an Indian untouchable. I don't know what I been thinking about all this time. I guess I was trying to . . . I don't know. Anyhow, tonight I felt so stupid, tonight I felt so goddam poor. . . ."

Frank brought his lips over his widely spaced teeth and blinked his eyes. His fingers came up and began fussing with the pens and pencils in his shirt pocket. For a few minutes he scowled at each of the four corners of his store. Finally he turned back to Angelo and cleared his throat; the sound seemed to startle him and he looked hurriedly at his fingernails.

"I'll make it five bucks now, and we'll talk about the other five later on," he snapped nervously.

A sad little grin touched Angelo's mouth. "You cheap bastard. You know something, Frank, you're one of the absolutes in the universe—you restore my soul."

"I got to do it that way for tax purposes and for my bookkeeping."

"Hey, *compa'*, I could almost love you," Angelo said.

"You're crazy, you know that? You're the craziest kid I ever seen."

"I know, *compa'*, let's forget it all for now." As abruptly as he had begun the conversation, Angelo ended it, and began taking things from the shelves and checking them off on his list. A sudden tiredness overlaid his features, an expression of tedium so magnified that it repelled all attempts to talk.

But after a few minutes, Frank could no longer bear the sadness.

"Hey, Angelo."

Angelo turned from where he was squatting beside a low shelf.

"You want to know the truth? If I *could* do something about what's really bothering you . . . I mean it's something worse than money, I know that. Seriously, kid, that other five bucks really wouldn't make any difference, would it?"

"I guess not, Frank." Angelo stared through his cousin with his mismatched eyes; Frank felt a shudder of some communicated terror.

"Aw, *Angelo*," he almost wailed as Angelo walked out of the store with the heavy carton. "Don't be a crazy bastard, will you? *Angelo . . .*"

In the children's pavilion, a small girl who had been in the hospital for over a year with first-degree burns, and who rode around the ward all day as though she owned it, bumped into him purposely with her wheelchair.

"Hey, watch where you're goin'," he said, scowling at the

glossy scar that ran up from her neck and raised her hairline by an inch at the temple.

"I want some ice cream." She had a bland, spoiled-looking face, and her chair was covered with toys.

"Too late—I'm delivering already. You got to wait till tomorrow. Besides, where would you put anything else on that float you're riding?"

"You're a ugly, mean man," she said, and stuck out her tongue.

"Sticks and stones." Watching her wheel off into the dim room, he felt the weariness and the boredom as acceptable conditions. Edges could be blunted; he could stop hurting himself. If he could get a better job . . . Maybe he would learn a decent trade and get a nice place to live. A better life was plausible: he could have time to read, go to the beach in summer; maybe he might even get to travel, on the off-chance that some places were a little different from others. As for sex, he had the poor man's harem—his imagination and the palm of his hand.

Minchia, he cried out in his innermost voice, I just want to ride instead of walk. I want clean clothes and an apartment to be by myself in. Probably that was all he had ever wanted; the ferocity of his quest for truth had been a deprived child's cry of arrogance. Okay, okay, he thought, lightening his load from room to room. I'll sell out, I'll take the route of the almighty buck, and someday I'll have a pair of Florsheim shoes, a Hickey-Freeman suit, a brand new Chevy, and my only questions will be about miles per gallon and how good flannel wears.

A senile old man, equipped with rubber plumbing in every orifice, called out to him in a frail voice, "It hurts like hell, it hurts like hell. . . ."

"Sure it does, pop," Angelo answered politely, without

116

stopping. And in the room where he delivered a hot-fudge sundae to a Negro woman as some small compensation for her amputated left breast, he looked courteously thoughtful when she sighed her complaint about the ice cream.

"I said vanilla. Chocolate ice cream just don't *do* it for me."

"Well, I tell you what. Tomorrow I'll bring you a free one to make up for it. How's that?"

"*Tomorrow,*" she said disdainfully.

His last item was a package of Tampax for a fifteen-year-old girl who was losing blood in several ways. She had the white, translucent skin common to tuberculars, and her fever spots enlarged as she paid him, her face averted. He counted out her change, hoping his rather gay manner was a manifestation of resignation and not of spite or cruelty; he despised cruelty because it was the face of weakness.

"And fifty-five, seventy-five, one dollar. We thank you," he said, smiling down at the part in her hair, grateful that her embarrassment did not affect him at all.

He walked out into the corridor. The empty carton was lighter than air in his hand. I'm learning to live with myself, he thought. And then he heard the gentle voice coming from the unlighted solarium.

"I'm back, *boychik*. Come break bread with me," Sammy said.

He could not know what moved him. Smell, sound, taste? He went, or was driven, or was coaxed into the solarium, and sat on the wheelchair next to Sammy's. The long, preposterous face held him; combers of feeling washed up into him, receded, came back again; vaguely, he felt his heart beating. He reached for his strength until his joints ached; there flashed into his mind a paragraph he had committed to memory: *The brain stem is essentially a bottle neck through which must pass the millions of afferent and efferent*

fibers connecting the brain neurons with the body as a whole.
And the heart? The only image he could conjure up was a
red valentine.

"So you're back," he said hoarsely.

"Like I never went away, *bubi,* like I never moved a inch."
What was it? Just a human voice, a little reedy, prone to
make small three- or four-note songs out of every phrase,
every sentence. And so tuned to the dark!

"And here in the hospital, they didn't make a fuss about
. . . you know, anything?"

"A leave of absence, just like if I had went into the army."
From the sound of his voice, it was possible to imagine his
smile. "You missed me, Angelo."

Angelo searched for resentment. "Well, I didn't figure you'd
be back," he said dully.

"Oh, I had my doubts myself, *totinka* mine. Like the cow
said after a day in a pen full of bulls, 'They seemed to want
me bad.' *Me,* especially me. It was like they had been through
a hundred thousand guys until they got to me, and their eyes
lit up. Howard didn't really interest them—another *faygele,*
they thought. But *me*—ahh." He slumped awkwardly in the
other wheelchair and glittered at the dark. "For days and
days they questioned and questioned. They told me, 'Jakey,
we looked you up and we know all about you.' They said,
'We found out you was once held on a suspicion-of-morals
charge.' They got sore when I laughed. You see, I remember
that time. It was at a beach near a town with a Spanish
name. . . ."

"Here or in California?"

"Either way." Sammy shrugged impatiently. "It was on the
beach near a big rock. I kissed a little boy and the parents
farted blood. So they arrested me and pushed me around a
little—nothing to it. Then they let me go. Really, though, you

should know the customs of the country, the laws. After all, they're only for your own protection, right, *bubi?* I should have known the local health laws—they only wanted to keep me hygienic. It's a terrible crime to kiss little boys here: here they're afraid of little children."

Listening to him, Angelo found a sliver of anger and seized it as though it were a solitary raft against his drowning. Yeah, Sammy, tell me more, you lousy clown, he said from the small perch of safety. Go on, go on, but I'll wait you out and I'll see you put away yet. Then I'll know up from down again.

"They said to me, 'You put it to that kid, didn't you, Jew-boy? You tried to put the blocks to a baby like that.' At first I said I didn't. Like the Bible salesman said to his wife when she complained about his switching over to selling dirty comic books, 'There's truth and there's truth.' And the more they said it and the more I thought about it, the more it began to seem that I *could* have done it, that inside me someplace, maybe I wanted to do something like that. I can do that—I can feel like anyone in the world, like *everyone* in the world. So it began to seem like I really did it, and I started to suffer for it. And finally I said that, yes, it was me. Can you imagine such a *meshuggaas!* So they punched me around a little—not too bad, just enough to keep them honest—and then they threw me in a cell.

"And I bumped around in there, like a man does. Did I suffer? Yeah, sure I did, but that was all right. I'd be afraid *not* to suffer. I worry when things are too smooth, I should get a *kainahurra*. Let me tell you the worst dreams of all for me. I dream like I'm God, up on top of everything with nothing higher. All I have to do is wave my hand and I got what I want. I got no pains, no problems. Hungry? I wave the hand and there's a roast beef. Everything. Nobody can insult me or beat me up or anything. I'm never cold or hot or sick.

But what is it when it's like the opposite? It *contradicts?* Because, you know, it's the worst, worst feeling I ever have. It's so lonely not to suffer, so *lonely*. Who would want it if they knew? I don't say I *like* to suffer or *not* like to suffer. But *not* to!

"Anyhow, I rolled around in that can, and when I slept I dreamed beautiful and miserable both. When I was awake I kept moving—I shouldn't gather moss. Pretty soon they send me a lawyer from the court, no charge. 'We got to plan a defense,' he says. 'You want to plead guilty on mercy of the court?' I said, 'What mercy? You went to school to be a lawyer, so be a lawyer. You want mercy of the court, so let it be mercy of the court.'"

He gazed at Angelo with an odd air of mischief; there was an air of wild scheming in the way he measured silence.

"I thought I was going to die and I said to myself, Samele, this life is an awful thing. How ugly you are, Sammy, I said. What a cesspool you are! But things are swimming around in you, things live on the *dreck*. And if you pull them up into the clean light, they die beautifully, and the cruddy fish in the cesspool look up from down in that *dreck* and they see a flash of light, dim, and they know one of their brothers is dying, but they hope that that's worthwhile, too. How does it figure? I got a low IQ and I think how nice it would be if Einstein could see it and make it clear. But I don't think that it's possible, I think that only *dreykops,* dopes like me, see those things. . . .

"Anyhow, all of a sudden, they come into my cell and they say I can go, that they found out it wasn't me at all, it was Lebedov all the time. But *was* it Lebedov all the time? Maybe when it was being done it was Lebedov, and maybe now it's Lebedov, but during that time when I felt it was me . . . Well, anyhow, here I am, back here. The Sister said I was welcome, that it was just a bad break and that I had my job still. But you know, *bubi*, I don't know what it all is, not in the least."

"You don't know," Angelo said sarcastically. "Hey, don't play with me. Your angles have angles. You're so sly that you fool yourself. You're a nut with a purpose, but who knows what it is? I say you're a comedian with more patience than I ever saw. And that's what makes you a nut, because no one in their right mind would take the trouble you took to con me."

"And how do you know so much, *boychik?*" The orderly's face looked pressed out and sickly; behind his smile there was a great weariness. "How do you know, for instance, that there's no such thing as magicians?"

"Look, Sammy, let's try and clear something. At your best you're an oddball, and I'll admit you got me kind of confused. Not because I really been influenced by your kooky stories and your weird jokes, either. Not that that's any compliment to me, because only a moron like Lebedov could have took them serious. No, but to be honest, you did mix me up, and I'm trying to figure out why. It's some kind of emotional thing—my own problem." He made a derisive, hissing sound. "Maybe I ident-tiffied you with my father, Dr. Freud. I don't know what, but I do know that the way I live could make me into some kind of neurotic if I wasn't straight with myself all the time. I mean I'm not even used to having a friend. Not that you're a friend—I don't know what you are to me. That's what bothers me because . . . because, the truth is, I admit it, you been bugging me plenty."

He could feel the mockery; the solarium seemed to belong to Sammy, and his quiet listening was like a playful forbearance.

"But let me tell you this: even though you got me mixed

up in some funny ways, I never stopped being clear about what really is. I'm an accident and so are you," Angelo said fiercely. "And whatever is queer about either of us is an accident too. I mean, did you ever hear of mutations?"

"*Never!*" Sammy declared, his hand over his heart.

"Go ahead, laugh all you want. I'll tell you anyhow. Mutations are the accidental changes that come in nature. A whole bunch of them over millions of years made apes into men. Them accidents made us into this certain kind of animal, animals who can be afraid of things we can't see. And because we're so scared, we got to invent stories to comfort us." He breathed heavily, admonishing himself against excitement. "Listen, it's just like the new cars with so many automatic things on them; they're more complicated, so more things can go wrong with them. What I'm trying to say is, there's no one to blame and no one to thank. I don't blame no one for nothing. We're just a poor design, that's all. It burns my ass to see people making big smoke clouds because they're afraid to face what they are. I'm sick of all this crap about 'suffering.' What do you think is so special about us? Christ sake, you don't find other animals carrying on like lunatics. We got a superior brain and we let it make us into a bunch of nitwits."

"We got a sense of humor," Sammy offered mildly.

"So do porpoises."

"Yeahhh, but not like mine." Sammy looked at the ceiling as though speculating on something that had just occurred to him. "You know, Angelo, I got jokes you haven't seen yet. Just hang around." He leaned forward in the wheelchair, so that it creaked slightly. "I'll break you up yet, kiddo, just wait."

"I don't want your jokes. You're plain ridiculous. I wish I knew why I even spend time with you."

122

"Maybe because you're lonesome and you don't have anybody else?"

"Who said I need anyone?" Angelo started to rise.

"Relax, relax, don't get so excited. Okay, maybe I'm wrong. Only I can't think of anything else," Sammy said innocently. "You tell me a good reason and I'll buy it."

"I don't have to give you any reasons. In fact, I can end it right now. You just get on my nerves." Angelo walked deliberately to the doorway, and for a wonderful minute he convinced himself.

"Wait, *bubi*," Sammy called after him in a calm, taunting voice; he seemed quite confident of his power. "I brung food for us. The least you could do is stay and help me eat it."

For a moment Angelo was afraid to turn around, and when he did so, it was with a sense of outrage and defeat.

"Yeah, *boychik*," Sammy said soothingly, pointing to the dim objects on the table. "A few cookies, some grape juice. After all, you got to nourish your body. Come, come, *bubi* . . ."

Helpless, Angelo went back and sat in the wheelchair. Slowly he began chewing on the dry cookies, his eyes fixed on the strange white face, sometimes lowering his head in the effort to swallow, but never lowering his eyes.

"And drink the juice with it, *totinka*, you're so thirsty."

Dutifully, Angelo drank, and his body and brain were dazed; it was as though something had been removed from him and something else put in its place.

"Ahhh, yeahhhh," Sammy brayed triumphantly in the night of the room.

CHAPTER TWELVE

HIS one day off and it had to rain. All morning he sat in his small room, unable to read, staring out at the drenched black ground and the wild, wet, cold-green bushes. He hadn't bothered to eat breakfast because that would have meant going out, and his hunger depressed him.

He sat with his arms up on the back of the chair, looking through the window, through the yard, seeing only surfaces. Absently, he chewed on the cloth of his shirt sleeve; the warm, wet, cottony taste brought him back to a remote summer evening when he and Theresa had been small children and relatives had come to visit Dominic and Esther. He and his sister had shared a bed, and he recalled the taste of the sheet in his mouth. Theresa had lain very quietly, sharing his breath and the unusual sounds of laughter in the yard. The men had sung Italian songs. He remembered being happy in the dark with Theresa beside him and the sounds of merriment coming through the warm evening; and he wondered if Theresa had any of that night in her unknowable brain.

After a while he began to walk back and forth across the room.

But this is suicide, pure suicide, he told himself. You have to fight rationally. Figure Sammy in some accountable way, and you can get rid of him for good, in one piece.

Suddenly, impulsively, he threw on his thin zipper jacket and went out. The rain on his head relieved him; he took a deep breath and headed for the hospital. When he reached it, he stood for a few minutes looking at the rain-darkened stone cross, and at the brick walls, which were soaked to a burned cordovan color. The building loomed above him in the gray air, its windows spuriously cosy with yellow light.

Inside, feeling shy without the sanction of his work, he moved uncertainly past the rooms. He had come because he knew there was no escaping what troubled him, but he had no way in which to look at the patients. They made him feel particularly vulnerable, and as he reached the junction of two corridors, he decided to leave.

Just then, though, there came a chugging sound as from a toy train, and Sammy appeared, pushing a cart full of bedpans, shuffling his feet and making the train sound with his mouth.

"Busman's holiday?" Sammy said, making the long *shhhhh* of the steam brakes as he stopped beside Angelo. "Okay, so I'll entertain you, come on with me, *bubi*."

Too worn down for scorn, Angelo followed him into the small room where the brooms and mops were stored. Sammy turned on the bare bulb light over the sink and closed the door behind them.

"This is better than television," Sammy said. "But you got to be absolutely quiet." He turned off the light, and fumbled obscurely. "There you go," he whispered. "Take a look."

Angelo moved to the postage stamp of light and put his eye to it. He was looking into a room where a man lay in bed and a woman sat in a chair beside him. He recognized the man of the painful belches, but there was a difference in seeing him like this. For some reason, the fact of Angelo's invisibility lent a special, shameful ugliness to the man, who looked much thinner and more worn. Nothing really went on: the patient dozed and woke and dozed again in short snatches of time. Yet Angelo's eye was held to the tiny aperture like a tongue to icy steel.

Each time the man woke from his short, deathlike dozes, he called the woman's name.

"Hetty, Hetty," he said urgently.

"It's all right, Sidney," she answered. "I'm still here."

The man seemed to be turning to wax: his hair, skin, lips, all had the same yellow-white color. Only his eyes, which were small and undistinguished, had a desperate sparkle, and when he came fully awake, he squinted as though to hide them from his wife.

"Lymphatic leukemia," Sammy whispered.

"Shall I call a nurse?" the woman asked, and smiled at the man. "No." The man smiled too, more broadly. "I don't need anyone but you."

She clasped his hand, and presently the terrible smile faded from his face and he drifted back into unconsciousness.

Angelo pulled away into the darkness.

"All right," he whispered. "What's the point?"

"Don't you think it's fascinating?" Sammy put the little

126

board back over the hole and turned on the light. "Didn't you ever wish you were invisible and could sneak into wherever you wanted? You see people like they really are."

"I think it's sick. It's like sneaking into a ladies' room. I'm no Peeping Tom."

"Ah, but you looked. And for quite a while." Sammy smiled and held out his hands. "You see? It's impossible not to look, it's impossible to ignore them."

"You don't have to smell their breath or touch their skin."

"Yes you do. For someone like you, that's what you have to do." Sammy turned abruptly away and began wheeling his cart through the connecting door that led to the kitchen-scullery, where he put the bedpans into a big, drum-shaped sterilizer and turned the steam valve on.

This room was larger and warmer. The steam hissed inside the sterilizer, the rain streamed silently down the window, and nothing could be heard of the rest of the hospital.

"So, *boychik*, what do you think?" Sammy leaned comfortably on the metal counter, staring with half-closed lids at the sterilizer; the fine hair of his head moved lightly in the airless room. "Because I tell you, I got things on my mind."

"What am I supposed to say to that?"

Sammy looked at him almost sternly. "Don't say a thing! You talk too clever and it's worse than being quiet."

"Fine. I'll let you do all the talking."

"Yeah, but will you listen? Will you really listen? What I mean is that I can't stand the way people are. They torture each other, they lunge at each other."

"And you," Angelo said. "What do you do?"

"Me?"

"Yeah, *you!* Listen, I'm not blind, I know about you. For one thing, I know that you been peddling drugs to the patients."

"Oh, that. See, you miss the forest because of the trees. I guess I misjudged you—all you really are is a little citizen at heart. You won't even try to listen to things that don't make a sound."

"Go on, go on, I won't interrupt. I'll be as quiet as an analyst."

"No, you see, I want to *do* something," Sammy said in a half whisper. "Always there's been something making me like crazy. I get like a huge, huge . . . thing, a thing I can't catch hold of. It makes me cry inside. I feel like making some stupendous joke because I can't think of any other way. I look at you and I want to do something terrible to you, something that will keep you from grinning like you do."

His voice became cleaner and higher. "See, I worked in hospitals for a long time. They're like railroad stations, with people saying hello and good-by. In hospitals—in hospitals you gotta take your skin off, you gotta love so much that you go insane or else turn cold like a machine. So maybe I'm crazy now, because this seems like the worst place I've been. Or maybe it's just that all the other places have added up and this is the last straw."

Angelo watched the rain running down the window.

"But I got a sense of humor, see—that's the one thing I've got going for me. So don't you have to use what you got? Hey, you should hear me with the Yiddish jokes. . . . Ah, but there's no point with you, you don't understand and they lose in English. It's a pity—there's some really great ones. . . ." Suddenly he grinned. "No, but you know what I'd like them to do?" He paused for a moment. "I'd like them to forgive Lebedov."

Angelo jerked his head from the window. "Whatta you want to do?" he cried. "Make the whole fucken world over?"

128

"Yeah. Yeah, *boychik,* that's what I had in mind," Sammy said with menacing softness.

Angelo stared at him for a long time. The sterilizer went off, and the rain beating in little gusts only added weight to the stillness.

"Who the hell you think you are?" he finally snarled.

"Ah," Sammy said, shaking his finger. *"Now* he asks. And why just me? Who is *anyone?* That's what you should have been asking all along."

"Look, let me try and get through to you, see if you can understand some very basic things. You rave away—'I got a secret,' you say. Maybe you impressed a lot of people that way, I don't know. But I do know a lot of other things, and nothing can confuse me about them. For instance . . ." Angelo's voice suddenly became monotonous; he was too pre-occupied with remembering what he had learned to give expression to his speech. "Thinking is the reception of sense impression, where certain pictures turn up in many different series of pictures, those pictures common to many series become the ordering elements, they connect series that are otherwise unconnected, when your mind advances from un-connected sense impressions to series that are connected by a concept, you have advanced from dreaming to thinking." Here he paused and became animated again. *"Thinking*—do you get it? Maybe you want me to translate it into Yiddish? You rave and rave, you talk in circles, and I listen. But do you know *why* I listen? Not because you're so clever, so *charming.* No, the plain reason is because I'm lonesome and I don't have nothing else to do. Sure, sometimes you get me kind of funny when I'm tired—I guess you got me sort of crazy like you a few times. But let me tell you this: I'll never fall for your shit, because I know what's really straight and true.

All your spooky talk isn't any mysterious cloud, it's a lot of dust. Well, don't blow it in *my* eyes. I can stand to see things."

"Okay, okay," Sammy said, holding up his hands. "So I'll entertain you a different way."

"Talk away." Angelo pushed himself up onto the counter and sat gazing at the window again. The incessant rain locked them in.

"I was born at a early age in a place called Brownsville, which is in New York. Of course, it was a mixed marriage—my mother was a woman and my father was a man. And you think *you* were poor! We lived in a cellar and ate two-day-old bread. My father was a ragman and we wore his merchandise, because of course we got it at cost. We were very religious—I can't begin to tell you. But it was a little weird because of how poor we were. For candlesticks we used ketchup bottles, and our *Shabbas* tablecloth was a white shower curtain. I used to have to wear a hat in the house all the time, but it was a good thing because it was very drafty in that cellar, damp too. We were white, damp people, I tell you—a family of mushrooms, and not what you'd call pretty. But except their eyes, my parents, their eyes. Their eyes were hot and dark and kept their faces warm. Yeah, and my father had two voices, two distinct voices. I used to think sometimes that he was two people, because he had the one voice to yell 'Raa-ags' and the other, which was soft and sweet, to *daven* and say the *Brochas* before meals. I never felt I knew him because of them two voices.

"Always I had ringworm or impetigo. Yeah, and I wore old curtains for clothes. . . . I remember my favorite was yellow with big lilacs all over—there was one blossom right over my crotch. I was tall for my age and my legs were like sticks. The kids used to like to push me over because it was so easy. Just a little nudge like to something that was barely balanced and over I'd go. They'd laugh like hell, too, because I was so serious—I was a very serious kid. They weren't malicious or anything, and they'd pick me up gentle and do it again. I never got hurt, but it seemed like I was dizzy my whole childhood from being up and down so much. I don't know what it was, they found the right role for me and that's how it stayed. Maybe they even liked me. After all, how could they know it hurt my soul?

"Besides, what a little thing it was in that neighborhood— one person's little humiliation; it was less than nothing there. People torment each other worse ways, much worse. With poor people it shows more, they actually do physical crimes. More civilized people can do to each other more refined, without lifting a hand. We had, for instance, in our building alone, two suicides and a murder. Up on the fourth floor there was a skinny house painter. It came out he was screwing his daughter. I know he was the saddest creature I ever saw—used to cry all the time, drunk or sober. I suppose he felt bad about what he was doing to his daughter. Or maybe it was the other way around: maybe because he felt so bad is why he did it to her. *Vair vayst?*

"In the winter it was cold as hell in that cellar. My mother dressed like the butcher's wife, who had to go in and out of the refrigerator: a man's hat, a couple sweaters, man's jacket, man's shoes, pants under her dress. Incidently, speaking of the butcher's wife, I remember something about her, clear as can be. Her kid one time was acting up in some way she didn't like, and she shoved the kid into the refrigerator for a while. I remember standing in the shop and watching, seeing the kid's screaming face but not hearing a thing from inside that thick glass. And I was shivering too, like the cold in there had got to me. I run out of the place, but after, I found out it didn't seem to hurt the kid because he came out and grew

131

up and got killed in the war. Somehow it stuck in my head, and I dreamed about it for years and years. Then again everything sticks in my head, everything. . . .

"Actually I had a fine home life; my mother loved me. No, really, what more can you ask? Of course, she thought I was a beautiful child. *'Mein ein unt einsick,'* my one and only, she'd say. But then you got to realize she had a astigmatism and we couldn't afford glasses for her.

"One Halloween a bunch of kids burned up my father's pushcart, and we all went outside and watched it burn. With all them rags it made a big blaze all right. It looked so strange in the night with everyone watching—religious, kind of. Everybody came out, they seemed to get a big kick out of it: it was like some kind of celebration. A guy even came around selling *knishes*. Look, didn't they used to sell refreshments at hangings? The fire lit up the front of the building and made it look like scenery. People whose faces I knew, they looked funny in that light—like savages or monsters. My father and mother stood watching like dead people, and they looked different too, so strange and different. . . . Afterward, when there was only little ashes and sparks, all the people went inside. My mother covered her head with her apron—some apron, a Pillsbury sack. I stayed out to watch my father *potchky* around with the burned pieces like he was looking for something, like the FBI looking for clues. All he found was a belt buckle, and he burned his hand on it. He looked at his hand in the dark, then he stood up and looked at me. He had a blue face and eyes like a guinea pig. He came to me and bent down and kissed me and then told me in his *davening* voice to go inside. Then he went up onto the elevated and jumped in front of the Pitkin Avenue train. Don't ask me to defend him—I'm just telling it.

"They took my mother to a hospital and me to a orphanage,

and I never saw my mother again. No, no, they weren't saints, my parents, they were too stupid to be saints. They only moved around by instinct; they breathed on me and touched me like I was Braille—we didn't know from love. Later I found out about that from the movies. In the orphanage nobody touched me, but I stopped wearing curtains and my diet improved. They said I had rickets and malnutrition, and they blamed my parents. They were nuts! My parents didn't give me rickets and malnutrition! All my parents gave me was their fumbly hands: I got their hands inside me to this day. When I was thirteen I got *bar-mitzvahed* in the orphanage and then I ran away. By then I had learned what a good sense of humor I had and I made my way fine. Yeahhh . . . it's a long story and it would take more than a lifetime to tell the rest. But that's the beginning—it should give you a idea.

"Obvious I'm a self-made man, but I'm still trying to find myself—you know, my calling. I got a feeling I'll find it soon, *bubi,* one way or another. There's a lot of things and they're all pushing at me. Of course, the longer it takes, the bigger I feel it has to be. By now I almost feel like I gotta kill someone to make it worthwhile. . . . So what do you think, *bubi,* what do you think of that?"

Angelo just shook his head and looked at the world in the rain. All over the earth a gray, teeming downpour fell on hair and flesh and wood and stone. And they were locked into themselves and only emitted these wailing, hooting cries, and haunted each other like wraiths who could not touch.

"It's still raining," Angelo said, as though in answer, or perhaps in surprise.

"So what can you do?" Sammy said.

"Let it rain," Angelo replied. He had a sensation of falling, disastrously.

CHAPTER THIRTEEN

"ANGELO, come in here," Sister Louise called from her small office near the lobby. "I wish to speak with you."

"Sister?" he said, entering.

"Sit down, please." She aligned the edges of some papers along the outer rim of the desk. "There are a few things I would like to discuss that relate both directly and indirectly to you."

He looked at her courteously. She might have been about fifty years old; her face had a disquieting effect on him because it was really very beautiful, but with the stony beauty of sculpture.

"Suppose we begin with what relates directly to you." Her

voice was hard as wire; she gave him a wintry smile. "This conversation was precipitated by your uncle and your mother. It seems that they were speaking to your parish priest, Father Marinelli, at St. Andrews. Whether they asked him to call me or whether it was his own idea I don't know. That is incidental. The point is that your family is concerned about you, and not without reason. Apparently you have left home and are living by yourself?"

Angelo nodded just perceptibly.

"In our rather lengthy conversation I learned much about you. Father Marinelli is a good man, and he is concerned about your ways."

"I only spoke to him two or three times in my life. It's amazing he knows anything about me."

"He has spoken considerably with your mother and your uncle. My feeling is that he sees you much as I do. And, knowing what I do about you, I can anticipate your resenting this conversation." Her face came as close as it could to amusement.

"Then why look for trouble, Sister?" His expression matched hers.

She permitted herself another cold smile and looked at her rosary on the desk. When the silence had matured properly, she went on.

"Your family are all devout, God-fearing people, and they are naturally concerned about your apparent spiritual emptiness. Since I see you so much of every day—you might say you were under my wing . . ." This time the smile was small and lemony. "I thought that since I had to speak to you about another matter, I might also take advantage of your time and . . ."

"Kill two birds with one stone," he supplied.

"You might say." That was as far as the smile could go

and she extinguished it. "Then, too, you are under some obligation to humor me, since I allow you to solicit here."

"My boss, Frank DeMarco, would be the one who was obligated, Sister."

"Let us not quarrel," she said, showing just a bit of her edge. "Tell me, Angelo, when did you make your last Confession?"

"I'm surprised Father Marinelli didn't talk to you about that."

She raised her eyebrows.

"I never made a Confession."

Very little happened to her face; if it were possible for stone to become harder, then you could say that her face hardened. "I don't quite understand."

"It's simple, Sister. I refused to go to church since I was a little kid. I don't know exactly what my reasons was when I was little, but I know I wouldn't go. My uncle used to whack me around a little to try to force me, but it never worked."

"I see," she said, looking at her fingers spread upon the green desk blotter. And then, *not* seeing, she raised her eyes without lifting her head; in the parochial school that expression had made her more feared than the nuns who slapped. "Are you not fearful about the future of your soul, Angelo?"

"No, Sister, I'm not."

"You come from a Catholic home. I cannot imagine what influences have made you this way."

"It is kind of funny," he agreed.

"You are not a Communist, are you?"

"No, Sister," he said smilingly.

For a few minutes she studied him, her eyes narrowing at the clever, indrawn look of him; her expression acknowledged that he was formidable.

"I'm sure that this is something we cannot resolve in a brief talk. I will have to ask that you speak to Father Marinelli at greater length. It seems to me that you take all of this too lightly." She leaned over the desk toward him. "You do, of course, believe in life after death?"

"No, Sister."

At that, she leaned over more, so that the desk edge cut into the undefined softness of her breasts, and it could be seen that her irritation was becoming excited into anger. "And the Trinity?"

"No, Sister."

"Jesus Christ, our Lord?"

"Sorry, Sister."

"Ohhh." For some odd reason her face seemed to relax slightly; it was as though that answer might have removed her responsibility. "What kind of a life must you lead, Angelo? I shudder to contemplate it—it must be quite empty and hopeless."

"It's no bed of roses, Sister," he admitted.

"Well, since you realize that," she said, apparently animated by the defeated sound of his answer, "why do you not seek help and comfort from Him whose solace is endless?"

"He just isn't there for me, Sister."

"You must summon Him with prayer and humility."

"That's impossible."

"Why do you say that?"

"Because I know better, Sister. And because I'm not humble and I won't bow down," he said, with the first hint of anger.

"You must accept help."

"I don't think we're getting anywhere with this, Sister Louise. Excuse me, but didn't you say there was something else you wanted to talk about?"

She took a fair-sized breath, moistened her lips, and looked down, restraining her irritation. "Yes, about your friend, the orderly, the Jewish man." Her voice flattened for a discussion of the profane. "As you know, there have been some dreadful disturbances here during these last few weeks. Mostly, of course, I speak about that appalling crime involving the Alvarez child. Now, there was no question in my mind that I had to give him back his job when he was revealed to be innocent."

Angelo paid attention.

"Obviously, in all fairness, we could not deprive him of his job just because of that unfortunate association. But he *is* a strange man. . . ." She gazed at the window for just a moment before returning her eyes to Angelo. "Certain things about him have disturbed me all along, nothing I could quite put my finger on. I have sensed a certain subtle upset among the patients. I'm not sure. Perhaps it is his quality of frivolity; one suspects an air of mischief in him. Oh, he is respectful enough, seems to do his work well. And yet . . ."

"Why you telling me all this, Sister?"

"I'm telling you because you appear to be friendly with him," she said sharply. "The point is, I do not wish to be unfair to him. As a result of misunderstanding, he has been through a most unpleasant experience. I would not wish to add to his bad fortune without good reason. But if there is any indication that he *is* an upsetting element here, why then I will of course have to dismiss him. I just thought that, as a friend of his, you would be interested in warning him."

Angelo didn't believe that her motives were altruistic; Sammy covered his tracks too well and she was the kind of person who insisted on evidence, even for herself. He didn't answer and she continued.

"There *is* one little eccentricity that has annoyed me," she said with a hint of slyness, as though she had read Angelo's mind. "I really could discharge him for that if I was not inclined toward charity. It seems he has been pestering some of the nurses and patients with a silly petition he has gotten up. To my knowledge he has been polite, but it *has* irritated people."

"What kind of petition?" Angelo asked.

"It asks everyone to forgive Lebedov."

"Oh." He sat back in the chair and looked at the junction of wall and ceiling. "It sounds very Christian to me."

Her face took on an almost lifelike color. "Don't be insolent. It only reveals your cynicism in all its pathetic aspect. I am suspicious of your friend's motives, and if I find something to act upon, I will let him go. I had thought—mistakenly as it turns out—that you might be able to influence him in a decent way. After speaking with you, I'm afraid it would only be a case of the blind leading the blind."

"I don't think I deserve this, Sister. I didn't do anything wrong except to disagree with you. You called me in here and somehow I disappointed you. I'm sorry, I just told you the truth."

"The *truth!* Do you *know* the truth?" she asked.

"I look for it, Sister—that's all I can do."

"You are presumptuous, arrogant, in supposing that you can judge the truth better than the Church."

"Sorry, Sister."

"Sorry Sister, sorry Sister—is that all you can say? You have the idea that you are above our nonsense. Oh, I have seen your type before. Perhaps you apply some impressive label to yourself, but to my way of thinking you are just morally lazy and weak."

Angelo got up, looking bored.

"You are able to justify all your selfish acts by some sort of perverse rationale. I wonder what excuse you gave yourself when you walked out on your family."

"I . . ."

"If you are interested, Father Marinelli told me that your sister is not well. He just mentioned it briefly—something about your exerting a strong influence on her. It's too bad. I wonder if she realizes what kind of boy you are."

"I doubt it, Sister," he said, in a cold, quietly savage voice. His temples throbbed from his effort to control himself. "You see, she's an idiot—she don't understand *anything*. She don't even know about Jesus Christ." He spun around and went out into the hall, shaking with anger. For a couple of minutes he leaned against the wall, digging his nails into his palms. Finally he took a deep breath, picked up the empty carton, and went outside.

He would have to stop by the house tomorrow, to see how she was. He knew what she could be like sometimes when he wasn't around.

If there were no Theresa and no Sammy, he thought, he could stand up quite comfortably to all the rest of them.

CHAPTER FOURTEEN

HIS mother greeted him quietly and without surprise.

"Are you all right?" she asked, with an intense stare. She had a dusting cloth on her head and wore her usual black dress; her eyes were hot and hungry, her mouth slack with misery. "You just walk out and forget us."

"What's the matter with Theresa?" he asked.

"She just lies around in bed all the time. She lost some weight, too, because she won't eat hardly a thing. It's because of you."

He walked past her to his sister's room.

Theresa lay on her side, with her knees drawn up to her chest; when she saw him, she made grabbing motions with her hands, but the lifeless expression on her face did not change. He sat on the bed beside her, and she pushed her head against his thigh and clung to his leg like someone clinging to a log in an empty ocean.

"All right, all right," he said. "It's okay." He could hear his mother pushing air through her throat as she stood in the doorway. "Why don't you eat your food, Theresa? Whatta you want to be bad for? See, your arms are like sticks—you'll get sick," he said, holding her frail arm. He looked down at her hair, which was as tangled as though it hadn't been combed since he left. He gestured toward it and looked sternly at his mother.

"She don't let me touch her," Esther said helplessly. "She's like an animal. I can't stand her when she's like that."

"Hey, Theresa, you listen to me," he said, pressing the soft skin of her arm. "I want you to be good. I want you to eat and do what you're told. For *me*. Try to remember, even when I'm not here. Even when you don't see me, I'm like here and you have to do what you're told. You have to eat and let Momma comb your hair. Look at me, Theresa, so I can know you're listening."

She sat up and looked at him. He tried to see into her eyes, into the tiny black holes of her pupils, to find his way into the darkness of her mind, where unknown pictures were developed in total night. He looked unrelentingly, but knew that all he would ever see was what his own brain created. Yet somehow he was convinced that she knew they both came from the same place. But did he feel more than mere obligation toward her? Surely there was no personality for which he could feel affection. What did he get from her? All there was between them was in himself. She fulfilled some need in him, and familiarity had magnified the need.

Facing him, her mouth slightly open, she let her gaze drift

142

up to his forehead and his hair. She was at her dim high point, and he couldn't bear the look of intensity that roved her face like a match flame moving behind her thin skin. He could have had almost the same relationship with a dog, except that, unconsciously, she took advantage of the fact that she resembled a human being. All people did the same.

"Come on, Theresa." He got up. "Let's go into the kitchen and have something to eat. But first I'll comb your hair, before you have birds building a nest there."

He combed her hair; then, in the kitchen, Esther gave them bread and gravy and glasses of *latte caffe*. She stood at the sink as they ate, watching her daughter's docility, and her face expressed her awe at Angelo's power.

Angelo observed his mother's pain and guilt. It was the same with her, he thought: she looked at her children with an attempt at love because all that she had ever read or heard, all that had been preached to her, had enjoined her to do so. She suffered because she couldn't tolerate her real feelings. Theresa and me are not lovable, he said to her silently. Relax, don't strain for it.

"I'll stop around every so often," he said. "Don't be afraid to call me at the store if she don't act right."

Theresa looked up at the sound of his voice.

"Keep eating," he commanded.

"You're so kind," Esther said.

He filled his mouth with bread to avoid a retort.

"Don't you want to come back?" Esther asked petulantly. "It's not right for you to live in a furnished room, it makes me feel bad. Besides, it's expensive—we're poor enough."

"I been sending you the same amount of money."

"Then you must be starving."

"Don't worry about me, I manage. The thing is, I can't come back here."

"Dominic isn't really mad at you any more. In fact he feels bad about you, I can tell. He walks around mumbling and cursing, much worse than when you were here. He's just too proud to tell you."

"*Proud?*"

"Well, ashamed, then."

"Let's leave well enough alone, hah? And another thing. Do me a favor and stop calling the nuns and priests about me. I had a real thing with this Sister Louise over at the hospital just because you called Father Marinelli and he called her. Said my family was worried about my 'spiritual life.' If it wasn't for Frank and the job, I would have told her to go to hell. Hey, do me a favor, hah? Just butt out, please? I don't want nothing from you or Dominic—just leave me be. I'm not sore at you or him, but I'm better off if you leave me alone. You don't have to feel guilty about me."

"I don't have to feel guilty," she repeated bitterly. "Isn't that nice of you? You're so *reasonable*. Do you know, you make my blood run cold you're so reasonable? I don't have to feel guilty. . . ." She shook her head and looked out the window; the wall of the next house limited her view. She narrowed her eyes and twisted her mouth upward in a parody of a smile. "You know, when I was sixteen, I was a pretty girl and I was happy. I can't even remember what it felt like. See, I *know* it was true, that it happened, but now it don't seem like it could have been. How can I describe . . . Like if it was something that I've seen proved by pictures. I see a pretty girl in a light dress and a ribbon in her hair, and under it someone has written, 'Esther Bove—1938.' I believe it, but it's . . . it's not *inside* me. Oh, I had dreams of a fine life, with a husband, and then children. . . ." She turned accusingly to him. "What happened to me? What did I do to deserve *this?*"

"You didn't do anything. It's all free—nobody has to earn it.

What I been trying to tell you, Ma, is that it's all a accident."

"Ohhhh," she gasped. "No, it's all right, only that you called me Ma, and I can't remember the last time you called me anything at all. It hits me like a knife." She turned her head away as though to hide a sudden nausea.

"Cut it out! I'm telling you it don't do any good. Things happen for no reason—we're unlucky people, that's all. Like we could have been born rich and I could have gone to college. Theresa might have been a movie star, my father could have been alive and healthy, Dominic could have been a intelligent man. Or, on the other hand, we could have been born Jews or niggers or Koreans or hunchbacks or not born at all. Could have, might have—what's the use thinking about it? *This* here is what is! I say the same things over and over, but it makes so much sense to me that I feel like convincing other people. So everything's a accident, so what? That don't seem too hard to take; it leaves things up to me. Just so long as I can see things clear, just so I don't have to take all that gas about Jesus Christ and Love and all the rest of them ghost stories. The thing is, I'm one creature and you're another, and the way things stand, we can't get anything from each other. Don't worry about being responsible for me. I release you. My advice is take off that black dress and put on a red one, and go out and find a man, because that would make some sense for you. As far as Theresa is concerned . . . Well, she seems to lean on me a lot, but that's not magic, either. She spent a lot of time with me as a kid—she's used to me, I make her feel secure, like. It's all very logical. Like they have this experiment with a dog, where they ring a bell just before they feed him. After a while he gets saliva even without the food, if they just ring the bell. That's Theresa. I mean everything boils down to something like that."

"Yes, sure, it's all so simple. Oh, in some ways you're a very smart kid. But you're a child in a lot of other ways. There are a lot of things that haven't happened to you yet. I'll never believe what you say, even if it does seem simpler, easier. Once you said, I remember it, you said that part of our brains is empty, so we filled it up with God? All right, maybe so—I'm stupid and I can't know those things. But even if you're right, if we ourselves fill our heads with God . . . well then, He's there. And what do you have, just the empty space?"

"I got to get back to the store," he said, standing.

Theresa pushed her glass off the table, and it broke into many small pieces.

"Theresa!" Esther shouted angrily.

"Take it easy, it was a accident," Angelo said.

"An *accident* again?" Esther said with a bitter smile. "Just look at her and tell me it was an accident!"

Theresa had raised her head almost proudly, and her eyes had taken on an unusual luster.

"You be good, Theresa," Angelo said. "I don't want you to do things like that. I *have* to go."

With her eyes directly on him Theresa picked up a plate and threw it crashing on the floor amidst the shards of glass.

"Oh Christ, Theresa," he moaned. "What are you trying to do?" He took a deep breath, bent down, and began helping his mother clean up the mess. Head to head, they worked, silently persevering beneath the girl's enameled gaze.

As he was going out the front door he heard something else breaking, but he didn't go back to see what it was.

That'd be all I'd need, he thought, to have Theresa come halfway to life. He hunched his thin, wide shoulders even more than usual.

That evening, Angelo didn't see Sammy, and it occurred to him that he might have holidays, too. He finished his work, helped Frank secure the store for the night, and then started for his room.

He had just passed a small Italian restaurant, about a block from the store, when he heard a moaning coming from about the level of his knees. Startled, he stopped and scanned the sidewalk. Then, just below the lighted window of the restaurant, in that utmost darkness that borders light, he saw something that he at first took to be a pile of rubbish. Slowly it moved upward, and the light caught a pale, human beak.

"Sammy?" he said, going over to him. "What happened?"

"What happened? A little discussion happened. Nothing at all," Sammy croaked. "Come, give me a hand, *bubi*." He held out his long, white-sleeved arm. "I've felt better in my life, but then again, I've felt worse."

Angelo helped him to his feet. In the light, blood showed on Sammy's face; it made Angelo's insides squirm.

"I got an idea you asked for this," Angelo said. "I bet it was all your fault."

"Maybe so, *boychik,* but some good came from it," Sammy said teasingly, his arm about Angelo's shoulder, ostensibly for support.

"Whatta you talking about?"

"Well, look how close it brung us together. Maybe I did it for sympathy?"

"Do you know what the best thing would be for everybody?" Angelo said from between his teeth. "For you to be put away! You don't do anybody a bit of good!"

But Sammy only threw his head back and laughed softly up at the dim, star-scattered sky.

They walked on together. After a few blocks Sammy directed Angelo up the steps of a narrow brick house that was joined on either side to others like it. In one window was a sign, "Rooms to Let," and in another an old, sun-faded service star from the time of the war. In the foyer were a number of dented mailboxes and jammed bell buttons; it was obvious that neither mailboxes nor bell buttons were in working condition, nor, in that house, did it seem that anyone would care. The walls of the foyer and of the hallway inside were heavily defaced with obscene words, initials, and crude pornographic drawings. There was a powerful cat smell and a lesser odor of insecticide.

As he helped Sammy up the creaking stairs, which were partly covered with tattered carpeting, Angelo found the words So this is where he lives, repeating themselves over and over in his brain. So this is where he lives, so this is where he lives. There was no sense or meaning to it.

On the second floor Sammy stepped away from his support and tottered into a room that had the metal letter and number 3B stuck on its door. After he had switched on the light that hung from the center of the high ceiling, he turned around with a gesture of invitation. Angelo stepped inside and looked at the room in astonishment.

The walls were covered with magazine and newspaper pictures of people—men, women, and children—in no apparent pattern or arrangement. There were nudes from sun-bathing magazines and girly books, and women in bridal gowns from the society sections of newspapers, and farmers and soldiers and prize fighters. There was a rotogravure of an African tribesman, the bloody figure of a man just beaten up by the police, a picture of a starving child, and another of little girls holding hands on a city street. There was an astronaut, and there was a Tuareg riding a camel past a lonely well. And hardly any wall showed through the collage of human faces. In some places the tape that held the pictures had unstuck, and corners moved slightly in the breeze, lending a surreptitious animation to the room.

"Make yourself at home," Sammy said, staggering to the bed and easing himself down on it with a groan.

A model airplane hung on a wire, nose down in a perpetual dive toward the pillow upon which Sammy rested. Angelo looked at him, framed by his weird room. Sammy's face was torn by bruises, and the red was shocking against the pallor of his skin.

"Some people can't take a little selling, they get all excited. Maybe I carry jokes too far?" he said mockingly, from a mouth that now had down-turned corners of dried blood. His eyes were tranquil under the mask of tragedy.

"I don't know how to talk to you," Angelo said. He found a cloth next to the small sink in the corner, and filled a pot with water. "Better let me wash them cuts."

"It's all right, it's all right," Sammy said to him with a careful smile that nevertheless split the new scabs beside his mouth. "I make good jokes, don't I, *bubi?*"

"You may be the champion joker of all if you keep up." Angelo began wiping at the blood on Sammy's face. Each touch of the skin gave him a dissolving sensation in his groin. I wouldn't make much of a doctor, he thought, watching how the water in the pot became laced with fine strands of scarlet when he dipped the cloth into it.

"Who beat you up, and why?"

"Ah, some guys. I made a few suggestions for their own good and they got annoyed. I think I *nujied* them too much." He seemed oblivious of the cloth moving over his wounds. "I got this little petition up. It just says that the people who sign this hereby express their forgiving of Lebedov—just a gesture. I thought I'd send it to Lebedov, make him feel good, like a get-well-soon card. I was trying to get these guys to sign. I guess it seemed to them that I just wouldn't take no for an answer."

"What's the point? You can't help Lebedov or anyone else."

"It's a beginning. If I keep going I may bring back *Gahn Eydem*." He laughed at Angelo's puzzled expression. "The Garden of Eden—Paradise!"

"The goddam nut houses are filled with saviors. They're a glut on the market. Hey, there's five times as many as there are Napoleons. You better try to snap out of it, before you go off the deep end. Can't you see what a pathetic . . ."

"People just don't realize," Sammy said in a musing voice. "I mean, go look at them talking, in palaces and laboratories and *buildings*. They get deeper and deeper in with their words, but they don't know. They got big cars, but they forget that they're so soft and frail that one teeny bump from their cars and they're nothing. They spend billions on fancy clothes, but underneath they're naked and only worth ninety-eight cents. They hide the earth from theirselves with steel and formica so they can forget that they're going to be buried in dirt. What they need is a big, big, tremendous joke to make them see the one little thing . . . that . . . How can they . . . No, but they got to remember Lebedov. He's a human —that's all there should be. There shouldn't be anything but people on this earth."

Angelo took the pot of bloodied water to the sink and poured it out, watching it run in a delicate pink stream down the drain.

"Maybe you think you're the Son of God," he snarled.

"We're all the sons of God, *bubi*."

"I hope, for your sake, you're joking." Angelo turned to face him. "There is no God."

Sammy considered that. "Well, then," he said finally, raising himself on his elbows and fixing Angelo with his crazy, mocking smile. "Then, *boychik*, I guess you would say we were all orphans together."

"And what am I supposed to do with a statement like that?"

"Do? Do what you want. Laugh if you want—I like to entertain."

"Goddam it, Sammy . . ."

"Oo-whoo-whoo," Sammy hooted. "How upset he gets!"

"You disgust me," Angelo said, staring around the room. "Either try to act human . . ."

"Human? What's human—like this?" Sammy swung his feet off the bed, crossed his arms, and assumed a ludicrously stern expression.

"Cut it out!"

"Cut it out? But that would hurt, *bubele*. Even with local anesthesia that would hurt terrible."

And then it burst from Angelo. "Leave me alone, you goddam freak!"

The stillness closed around his cry. Sammy continued to smile, but he moved his lips helplessly, like the gills of a stranded fish.

Feeling a profound hurt all through his body, Angelo looked at the living face silhouetted against the patchwork of photographed faces on the wall. It was a caricature, stained and comic and mad. The street was quiet: the most distant sounds were amplified and came with the nostalgia of distance. And the two of them were arrested in the stillness, each breathing slowly, with dedication, as though breathing were their only reason for existing.

"Do you like people to be forced to insult you like that?" Angelo asked wearily. "Don't you have any pride you're a man?"

"Pride in my manhood? Yeh, sure, *boychik*. Like I'm proud that I can pee standing up."

"You know, you're hopeless."

"That's what I mean."

"Hey, just tell me one thing, hah?"

"Name it, *totinka*."

"Whatta you want from me?"

"Everything," Sammy said. "That's all." He held out the crumpled scroll of paper he had been holding all the time. "You want to sign my petition?"

Angelo spun around and ran out of the room, down the stairs, into the humid street. He never stopped until he was in his own room with the door closed behind him.

He thought, he stared, he moved his lips in silent debate. Finally he seemed to have arrived at a serviceable composite of facts, and he sat down and block-lettered a note to the chief of staff of Sacred Heart Hospital.

THIS IS TO INFORM YOU THAT A CERTAIN ORDERLY BY THE NAME OF SAMMY HAS BEEN MONKEYING AROUND WITH DRUGS THAT HE SHOULDN'T HAVE. HE HAS BEEN GIVING THEM TO THE PATIENTS. HE SHOULD BE LOCKED UP.

He folded the paper neatly and put it on top of his wallet, where he would remember to take it and mail it in the morning.

CHAPTER FIFTEEN

SUPPER hour and early evening light. He lay on his bed, reading. That morning he had mailed the letter—it might have arrived already—and now he felt nothing.

Islanded in the soft sounds of supper dishes and the burble of children's voices from a distant yard, he did the one thing, wholly. A cheap alarm clock made a picket fence of sound that surrounded his own silence. No one was with him in any way right then. He was a prone figure with sunlit legs, an open receptacle for the precise complexity of the printed page.

Through a beautifully co-ordinated oarlike beating movement of these cilia, the ciliated animal is able to move about in search of food or of more favorable environmental conditions. And cells with essentially the same type of ciliary action . . .

Outside the ticking room, people lived noisily. A man's raucous laughter disintegrated into a coughing he might die from; a woman squealed a long "Nooo-ooo" to him or to someone else. The leaves hissed and boiled in a breeze that swung the tiny ring on the cord of the window shade. The ceiling creaked overhead; water groaned and bumped through the pipes in the walls; sunlight presently stopped slanting through Angelo's window.

All the vital processes enter in the cell as the fundamental unit of structure and function, and all are bound up with the fact that the living state . . .

The alarm rang.

"Crap," he said, getting up from the bed, into the stupid chaos.

In the store, still slightly winded, he said to Frank, "Did you know that the energy for life comes from the sun?" His voice was uncharacteristically wistful; he tore off the piece of cash-register paper without really seeing what he was doing.

"So big deal. What am I supposed to do?" Frank said gruffly.

"So, so the sun is going down and I don't have no energy. Why don't you give me the night off?"

"Ho, ho, ho. Is that from a smart guy? You read a lot of books. How come you never read economics? Even scientists got to eat. See, that's *my* book—the economics. I give you the night off and I violate the book. You left off a couple steps when you said the sun gives energy. The sun gives the tomatoes energy, then you have to get the money to buy them and eat them, *that's* how the sun gives you energy."

Watching him laugh, Angelo thought Frank might be right. He fussed around among the shelves, procrastinating. In the most powerful way, he just didn't want to go to the hospital: there was something terrible over there. Or maybe it was in himself. Or, most likely, it was in both places and he carried with him the catalytic agent that would unite and explode both of them.

"Whyn't you get going?"

"I don't feel so good, Frank," he said, without sufficient guile.

"What're you trying to pull?"

"No, really."

"What hurts?"

"What hurts? Oh . . . my chest, my back. I think I'm coming down with something."

"You look okay."

"Appearance is deceiving."

"Yeah, sure, I'll say it is," Frank said caustically. "You just take a couple aspirins, and when you're through with the hospital, I'll let you off."

"You're all heart, Frank."

"That's what I tell you. Stick with me and you'll be *o*-kay."

"Sure, Frank," he sighed. "I'll stick like glue." He put the pencil behind his ear and walked slowly to the doorway, where he stopped and turned a blind look on Frank—the hopeless look of someone being devoured from within. "Help me, Frank?" he said.

"What's the *matter*? What is it?" Frank asked in genuine alarm. "If there's really something . . ."

Angelo smiled. "Oh no, nothing. Just that I'm so fucken poor," he said.

"Hey, wait a minute, Angelo," Frank called, coming out

155

from behind the counter. But Angelo was gone, and there was nothing Frank could hope to do for him.

Angelo went into the hospital and began working his way up, surprised at the narrow range of the orders; everyone thirsted and the variety on his list was only in the flavors.

The pimpled youth in the remote room had an alkaline whiteness on his lips, as though he were passing through a desert.

"I drink water and more water," he said. "What's good for thirst?"

"Lemon," Angelo said. "Lemon is good for thirst."

"Then gimme a lemonade, the biggest lemonade you got." He shaped the size of his desire with nail-bitten fingers, his face scourged by illness and a thirst he would never alleviate. "Whatta you do when you're through working?" he asked, and then didn't wait for an answer. "Do you bowl? Maybe you go to the movies? Shit, I love the movies! I stare at these walls and I think about *Ben Hur*. Man, that was a movie! Or *Solomon and Sheba*, where that whole friggen army went crashing into the ravine. Oh boy, if only someone would show that on this here wall, Jesus, would that be great! You know, sometimes I think I'll *never* get out of here. Hey, where is that Sammy? If you see that guy, tell him I need him, will you? You know what I mean."

"Yeah, I know what you mean." Angelo waved his way out of the room.

When he stepped into the second-floor ward, he was shocked to see Sammy. But had he expected his little note to make him disappear from the face of the earth? It would be all right; it was out of his hands. Things would be better all around. He slipped inside and went to the last of the fourteen beds to begin taking orders, his eyes on Sammy, who was bent over a man swathed like a mummy, feeding him and talking steadily.

The patients were eating, but their eyes went from Sammy to his cart and then back again, their faces curiously peaceful. Sammy's expression as he spooned food into the helpless man made Angelo think of a movie screen after the film has finished and the white light of the projector shines on it with a strange quality of divorcement and emptiness. Presently, humming some unrecognizable tune, Sammy wheeled the cart to the end of the ward and began scanning the beds and tables; when he at last noticed Angelo, he only shrugged, oblivious, serenely lost in some private domain.

"Welcome, *boychik*," he said, spreading his long, long arms. "These are my people—they have afflicted bodies. They're afraid of living and afraid of dying. They want me to help them, but they won't admit it. I mean, what can I do?"

"You can shut up," said a red-faced man with lumpy features who was obviously in some kind of pain. "That's what you can do."

Sammy turned his palms upward and rolled his eyes. Two of the patients turned over on their sides, sulking like children. The others watched him without clear expression.

"I tell them, 'Look, it's all an accident—you know, with heredity and all.' I tell them, 'You got organs and they get beat up one way or another. I mean, there's answers for all of it,' I say to them. But, *bubi,* they keep looking at me like I'm lying, like there's more, like maybe I'm holding back the punch line. They say, 'Make me happy, Sammy, *Ich bin kronk.*' It's like they think I'm hoarding from them."

"Why don't you shut up," said the red-faced man. He spoke with his back to Sammy, but the pitted flesh on the nape of his neck expressed his anger. "Why don't someone get him out of here?"

"See what I mean," Sammy said. "What can I do for *him?*"

Angelo, pretending to ignore him, went on taking orders. The hospital cart glinted in the late light like ancient pewter, and Angelo made terse commerce with the bedridden men while the high, ludicrous voice slowly filled the room.

"I mean," Sammy said to Angelo, to all of them, perhaps to himself. "A woman may work from sun to sun, but a man's work is never done. What a life, what a life, hah, *kinderlach?* Hey, I'm only here to entertain you—a song, a dance *efsher?* Maybe a little one-act play? Only a short stand, of course, because I got a lot of other rooms to play. That is, unless you hold me over. I got something for everyone, no one loses. And the price of a ticket? Just one thin dime in the plate or *ein tollah.* . . . Or maybe just a couple tears? Come on, come on, forget your *tsoris,* Sammy is here. *Kvetch* out your pain into the sterling bedpans, I'll relieve you. You'll just *think* of these magical bedpans and it'll comfort you. We'll hang a bedpan on every wall, and you'll remember me, you'll remember me, you'll look forward to the next time I come around. Because I love you all, you hear? Nothing turns *my* stomach. I'll kiss your gallstones, your ulcers, your cancers, your bleeding piles—and they'll all disappear! It's all psychosomatic anyhow and I'm the miracle man. I cure snakebite, dt's, dropsy, broken hearts—from angina, of course. Let a laugh be your umbrella . . . da, da, da, dee, dee . . . Hey, did you hear this one? He was carrying the cross down the street, crowds all around, soldiers in front of Him, soldiers behind Him. Two guys were watching, and they noticed He was moving His lips, muttering something. So they get up close to hear, and what do you think? He was singing 'I Love a Parade.' Hah, is that something? You get it, hah? Am I a comedian or am I a comedian? Oh, hey, I got a million jokes, a billion."

Now the windows were the color of smoky pearl, and still no lights had been turned on in the ward. Through the branches of a tree, Angelo could see the early evening sky; there was a somber ridge of cloud, so sharp-edged on the pale blue that it looked like cast iron. He could sense it rising like a lid over the city as the air sucked slowly away. The room was silvery. All around the tall, gawky figure, the patients exuded an atmosphere of anger and ecstasy.

"Gimme a coffee soda," said the man with the yellow, hairless face of a llama; he suffered from a ruptured spleen. "And a package of Oreo cookies." As he spoke, he looked past Angelo to the white performer beside the pewter cart.

"Look how I'm balancing," Sammy called out, so happy he almost sobbed. "Ain't I a marvel! The earth is rolling a thousand miles an hour and I keep my balance. Gravity, sure, okay. But then, why was I born? Oh, sure, because my father, the ragman, was weary and sad and he turned over in bed, and there was my mother, who might have been beautiful in the dark. But why were *they* born? Same thing, and back, and back, and back, and back—to the beginning. Eh, it's all a dream, *with* neutrons."

There was a low rumbling all around. Angelo knew he was being mocked, that all of them were, but in such a wild and monumental way that their oppressor was beyond retaliation. He felt the anger rising as the window turned darker. A hot breeze flew in. The red-faced man pushed his call button furiously. *Did* Sammy know he had been betrayed? Angelo bent himself as though to hear the murmured orders—but really it was pain that bent him.

"The September issue of *Factual Detective*," the old diabetic said, envious of the sweet drinks the others ordered. "Make sure it's not August, because I read August."

Angelo went on to the next bed, speaking softly, to all appearances armored against the madness in the center of the room; he knew that it had to end soon now. "And what'll you have, Mac?" he asked, his voice as frail as a harmonica played in the presence of an enormous waterfall.

"And here's the puzzle, ladies and gentlemen. Find the people. Take a room, any room. There, see, I'm not peeking. Or a restaurant, a fancy apartment house, a theater, a hospital room, even a space rocket. Okay, what do we see? Concrete, wood, glass, paint, metal, cotton, wool, plastic. Oh, but there—see those tiny little soft things sticking out the ends of clothes? You know what they are? They're *faces!* And even some of them are hidden by glasses and masks and like that. And what do those creatures have inside—love? We'll make it cheaper from plastic, it'll last longer, too. A bargain, formica hearts in all patterns—marble, spatter, terrazzo—and in all colors, coral, magenta, French blue.

"No, what I'm saying, don't you get what I'm say—See, you don't have a chance without signing the petition. I got here insurance, a down payment . . . How dark it gets! And when we're all in the dark—what then? Nothing? Never mind, never mind, Sammy will kiss it, make it all better. . . ."

Now several of the patients began shouting and pressing their call buttons with all their diminished strength.

"Get him out of here!" the red-faced man cried, but the others just lay back weakly, perhaps wondering if this was the way one died.

"Listen, listen, there's a lot you're liable to be missin'. . . . I mean, do you all see what Sammy sees? Is my red your red? Oh my God, I'm scared for me! I'm so alone up here! I never, never touched a woman in my whole life. But I *wanted* to. . . . Such dreams I had about them! Oh, I'm so high—I wish I could come down to you. Wow, wow, isn't this the end?"

Now everyone was silent. Angelo felt a core of ice shaping the inner surface of his body as he looked at the huge eyes; they were like bottomless pools of clear water, but strange because they grew no darker with depth.

"Isn't it all a joke? But will I wake up? Spinning out here . . . I mean, a dime a dozen, hurray for the flag, watch out for perverts, and there's a ten per cent, so we got to calculate . . . calculate. . . . But O close your eyes, close your eyes and listen to the nothing and then scream and scream and scream, just to hear the echo. . . . Because we all have to hold hands in all this dark. . . ."

Suddenly the overhead lights went on, and a nun, a nurse, and McKenna were standing in the doorway.

"All right, Sammy, all right now," the nun said gently. She was the rather sweet-natured nun named Sister Cecilia, and Angelo wondered how she could maintain her gentleness in the light of what she must know about Sammy now. "Why don't you just go down to Sister Louise's office and we'll talk down there."

There, all over now, no more problem . . . Angelo waited for his body to loosen, but it stayed frozen. His note had been delivered; it would be taken care of. His body remained locked. Where was the thing that could thaw him?

Sammy looked exhausted and his smile was ghastly. "Ah," he said, staring through the nun. He began pushing his cart out of the room.

"Just leave it here, Sammy, we'll take care of it," the nurse said, nodding at McKenna, who slid the cart away from Sammy.

Sammy shrugged and kissed his hand. Then he moved weakly to the door. And when he was gone, Angelo went back to taking orders. He was trembling and cold; the ends of his fingers had no feeling and he dropped his paper twice;

but it didn't seem to matter. Maybe now there can't be any more, he thought.

Sister Louise called to him as he was passing her office on the way out of the building.

"Have you seen him, Angelo?" she asked. "He never did get here. I'm surprised Sister Cecilia sent him off by himself."

"I didn't see him," Angelo told her.

"I suppose I'll have to get the guard to look for him."

"I suppose so," he agreed.

"The guard will find him," she said to Sister Cecilia, who had followed her out of the office.

"I guess I'll wait around until he does," Angelo said, and when Sister Cecilia questioned with her eyes, he shrugged. "Naturally it bothers me," he said. "But don't ask me why," he added.

"I believe that your friend is a sick man," Sister Cecilia said. "It has been brought to our attention that he has done some criminal things, but I don't think he is responsible for his actions."

"There's no doubt about that," Angelo agreed, too reasonably.

"We'd like to help him if we could," Sister Cecilia said.

"The feeling is mutual," Angelo said, "because he'd like to help *you* if he could."

Sister Louise just stood there, in a strained patience.

"It must have been a very trying experience for you," Sister Cecilia went on, valiantly maintaining her sweet expression. "Being friendly with an unfortunate creature like him. I mean, a youngster like you . . ."

"Yes, Sister." He was suddenly very tired again.

The hospital guard appeared down the corridor with a flashlight in his hand, and when he came abreast of them he shrugged. "Boy, Sister," he said peevishly. "There's five floors, two wings, the children's pavilion, and two basements."

"Well, you just keep looking," Sister Louise said.

"I'll need help, Sister. I mean, he could dodge me for a week down in them basements."

"If you haven't found him within the next few hours, I'll call in a city policeman to help you."

"It's not that I *mind* doing it myself. It's just that . . ."

"Yes, yes," Sister Louise said impatiently, waving him away. When he was out of sight, Angelo asked if he could wait in the office. "And could I use your phone to call my store?" he said.

She gave him an exasperated nod, and waved at the telephone.

"I'll be here for a while," he told Frank. "Something happened and I want to stick around."

"What do you mean, something happened?" the jaybird voice squawked into his ear.

"I can't tell you over the phone. I just gotta stay." Looking at the air, his voice becoming vaguely plaintive, he said, "I told you I didn't want to come here tonight. But now I'm here and I got to stay, Frank, I got to stay."

"Okay, *compa'*," Frank said, after a silence. "You do what you have to. Just try and take it easy, hah?"

"Yeah, Frank, okay." Angelo hung up, and sat on the old wicker-backed couch.

The two nuns murmured in the doorway. Finally, Sister Cecilia went away and Sister Louise came in and sat down at her desk. Angelo began riffling through the pages of an old copy of *Life*.

Inside and outside, everything was still. The trees stood motionless, waiting for a storm; the hallways filled with silence; Sister Louise rustled papers at the desk. What was he waiting for? He had become a stranger to himself, and he was filled with mistrust and fear of that stranger.

I am what I am, whether rotten and stupid or what, and I never asked for anything. It's a hard life, but I never used to cry about it. Why this? Christ, I hardly escaped a rubber, and if I had my choice, then I might have chose to go down the toilet with billions of others. I don't complain, because there's no one to complain to, so this don't make *sense!* What's happened to me, that's all I want to know. Two months ago I wouldn't have sat here like this. Two months ago Theresa didn't bother me, and even now I know she's got the mind of a weed. But *him,* that maniac sneaking around down there someplace. His brain is like rotten wood, and the jokes he dreams up are so crazy and private that no one but him could appreciate them. How can I let him drive me out of my mind? It's ridiculous. But I actually feel *sick,* sick as hell. . . .

He sat on the couch, kneading his hands, while the white, crazy face burnished his brain, and he felt something stretching dangerously inside him. Damn it, damn it anyway, he said to himself.

"You must be pretty busy, Sister," he said. "You're here so late."

"I have my work."

"I guess it's good that you do," he said innocently.

She looked up at him. "There is something very strange and bad about you," she said. "You don't believe in anything, do you?"

"I believe I'm alive and that things happen." He looked intensely at her. "But he bothers you, too, don't he? I mean, this seems to upset you, too."

"Of course it does. First the awful thing with the child and Lebedov, then this. This man is ill. We have discovered that he was stealing drugs, opiates, and selling or giving them to the patients. You say, 'It bothers you,' as though there were something strange in that." She passed her hand over her face, a nervous and uncertain gesture. "There is something quite wrong with this conversation. I don't know why I . . ." She put her hand down and sat more erect. "I have so much work. I wouldn't be surprised if you were a disturbing influence around here. I must speak to the chief of staff about this arrangement. I really would like to know who first allowed the concession to Mr. DeMarco."

"But I didn't do anything wrong, Sister. What do you have against me?"

"It's your attitude," she said.

"Sister?"

"You don't love God!" It burst from her in a frightened cry, and she looked at him from a depth of embarrassment and hatred.

"How do you know about what I love?" he said angrily. "Any more than I know if there's any love in you!"

"How dare you!" she said, standing up. "This is too much. I must ask you to . . ."

"Oh, Sister," a nurse called from the doorway, her expression rigidly casual. "Could you come to the third floor right away? We're waiting for Father Piermonte now."

"What is it?" Sister Louise said sharply.

"It's that little Alvarez girl, Maria. You know pneumonia set in a few days ago? I believe she's dying, Sister."

"Ohh," Sister Louise sighed. She turned an unfathomable expression on Angelo. "Yes, yes, I'm coming," she said, and followed the nurse out.

After a while, Angelo slid down on the couch and closed his eyes. Sleep began to seem possible.

"Now hear this, now hear this," the loudspeaker blasted into the quiet.

"Now hear this, now hear this . . ." A muffled cry from someone was followed by frantic calls too far away from the microphone to make out; and then, clear and unhurried, in Sammy's high, clinging voice, *"Yis-gad-dal v'yis-kad-dash sh'meh rab-bo . . ."*

There was a fluttering sound. A woman's voice cried, "No, he went that way." Then silence.

He woke to the hard reality of sunlight. The room was clear, down to the dust shadows and the nap of the rug and the grain of the wooden desk, behind which Sister Louise sat writing. Someone had covered him during the night.

"Thanks for covering me, Sister," he said.

Weariness had refined her beauty even more painfully, and she looked quite brittle. "I did not cover you," she said. "It must have been someone else."

He made a silent O with his lips and looked up at the wall beyond the crucifix. The window was open, and the air was fresh after the night's rain. The wetness rose, sweetened by the battered grass and shrubbery. Carts sounded in the hallway: breakfast was being served and fresh linens brought up from the laundry. Footsteps went in every direction as the nurses and internes changed shifts.

Could he have slipped in while I was sleeping? he wondered with an odd chill. He sat up and looked at the blanket. It was the ordinary hospital issue, gray with the maroon words "Sacred Heart."

"Did they find him, Sister?" he asked. "And how is the Alvarez girl?"

"I think it is about time you left here. This is all very irregular, as though we were running a hotel." She spoke with her head bent toward her endless paperwork. Then, with her eyes still downward, she said, "No, they did not find him. I wouldn't be surprised if he had left the building long ago." She waited again. Finally she looked up at him, her skin ivory in the morning sun. "The child is dead," she said.

"Oh." He pushed his hair back with combing fingers, quite fragile himself. "That's too bad." He hoped no one would shout or drop something heavy, because he knew it would do him incalculable harm. "But of course you can't blame him for that."

"How can you *say* that?" Her anger seemed almost worn out, though. "I saw and heard the wild ways he talked to Lebedov. What could you expect when you arouse a creature like Lebedov?"

"Lebedov didn't understand anything he said."

"Could anyone have understood that man's ravings?"

"No, no, I guess not, Sister. But just the same . . ."

"What are you trying to say, boy?"

"Only that nothing is anybody's fault."

"What a dreadful thing to believe! Why, if that were true, life would be terrible. There would be nothing but agony." She seemed tired enough to be hurt badly, and he could not resist the cruelty.

"That's what I mean," he said.

"Jesus Christ died to redeem all of us. . . ." Her words rose to a questioning tone.

"I don't know anything about it—that was two thousand years ago."

"There has been no other decent man since then!" she cried fiercely, and then held her breath, with the humiliation of someone who has answered a revealing question that was not asked.

Angelo somehow knew that he had sold her in part on his

167

view, but, strangely, he had discovered that all of this was infinitely worse than he had imagined; she had opened him to even more pain, too.

Somewhere in the building, he was certain, Sammy was appallingly tired. What was he waiting for? What grotesque fancies would move him to come out? Only let him come quietly, quietly, he begged. Let it be done gently and then be over with. He felt as though he had never slept, and he stood up gingerly.

"*Will* you please leave now?" she asked plaintively, like a woman. "I am so very tired, and talking to you gives me pain."

"Sure, Sister, I'm going. Thanks for the couch."

She just closed her eyes to him and he went out into the hallway, where there was movement and sound. Two policemen were in the lobby, dirtying the cleaned ashtrays with their cigarettes. Even the weak voices of the patients sounded cheerful. He headed for the nearest door.

Nurse Sullivan approached like a childhood dream; she seemed much younger than he. Her hair was glossy and innocently curled from last night's home permanent, her face bright with colors she chose herself.

"You look a hundred years old, Angelo," she said in passing.

"You're very close," he answered without stopping, anxious for the outdoors.

CHAPTER SIXTEEN

FROM the emergency entrance Angelo could see the whole
length of the building. To his left were the backs of the old
brick houses where the student nurses lived; beyond them rose
the tall white mass of the new building. To his right were
the other two entrances that faced on the yard, one parallel
with the emergency entrance, the other at a right angle, so
that it faced the entire cement area between the main building and the children's pavilion.

Perspective was altered by the unusual clarity of the morning air. Mica in the cement glittered from the pavement and
from the mortared lines between the old bricks of the buildings. The sky was a hard, unreal blue; the trees might have
been carved jade.

At the entrance that faced the length of the yard there were iron railings beside the steps, and on either side of the bottom step was a blunt, ornate spear, which, like the railings, had recently been painted black. The two huddled women and the man who were now ascending the steps seemed afraid to touch the iron because the paint still looked wet. The women were dressed in black and the man held himself like a shaft of glass. A priest and two nuns stood in the doorway, patiently waiting for them. But they were very slow, stopping on each step; it seemed they would take a long time to reach the top.

Angelo looked away from the tedium of their movement. The sunlight picked tiny, irrelevant places to explode: on the brass railing, a pane of glass, a chip of silica, a dime-sized puddle of water. Everything that moved did so with the pomposity of a pageant. And the quiet! Some patient's radio that was actually turned down to the prescribed volume could nevertheless be heard throughout the yard, playing the saccharin organ theme to a soap opera. A slight wind came up, and teased a scrap of paper down the concrete. The people reached the top step at last. The radio was shut off suddenly. The piece of paper stopped, and settled. For an instant, nothing moved.

Here he comes.

Sammy.

All dressed in white, but not so white now; crumpled, soiled, his fly open. So unimpressive with his long, silly Jew face, his tall ungainly figure, his boneless walk. His hands were out, palms upward, and he was talking, but Angelo could hear only his voice at first, not the words. He had come out of the entrance between Angelo's and the one that faced the yard, the one whose steps the three people had just ascended, and he headed for it immediately. Angelo walked after him; he was quite close when Sammy turned his face up to the mourners—close enough to hear what he was saying.

"No, no, you don't understand," Sammy called in his high, demanding voice. "I'm only saying to forgive him. I'm only saying to love him. And me too."

For an instant Angelo considered trying to stop him. But then he saw Sammy wink, and he held himself back. Oh, go ahead, Sammy, there's no stopping you.

"Come on, folks," Sammy cried. "Come on, say you forgive him, because I love you, love you, love you. Hey, we're all ninety-eight cents' worth of *fleish*—I mean we don't have a ghost, otherwise. We'll all blow up, *bada-boom!* No, don't look at that new building, that don't help. You can't go burning up the pushcarts and the fairies and the *kronk* ones, because you'll burn up your own guts and bellies and cocks. . . . *Oy vay,* what a way! *I* forgive Lebedov. I forgive you. I mean it's only the *one* child. Come on, come on—you have to." He moved up the first step and then the second, casting as black a shadow as anyone else.

"Like women, juicy flesh, big soft tits and nipples. *Ah zuchen vay,* what a day for the race! Love one another, love me, love you. . . ."

He went up the third and then the fourth steps. Ambulatory patients peered out of the nearer windows; orderlies and custodians stopped the little they were doing to watch; in the children's pavilion, the small heads were one to a window.

"What is it otherwise, *kinderlach?* Alone all nasty, alone pain shit dark and *nothing!* My mother and my father . . . The old, old way, and all you have is the end. So how about it, see? Old Lebedov, ain't he the hot one! Oh, he's in it now. Cool him. Coo-o-o-l him, baby. . . ."

A flapping scarecrow, his arms waving, his body coming to roost in the bright hospital yard. What is he selling, hell or the other? Some dim Spanish curses coming from the bereaved father on the porch—too small to bother about. The priest objects silently from the doorway, paralyzed by some extreme. Oh, forget them all, Sammy, upstage them all—yeah, yeah, go ahead, it'll all be downhill afterward.

"It's here and now!" Sammy shouted. "You can touch me and I can touch you. It won't be any better. Love me, O *kinder!*"

His bony arms reached out toward the father, and there was a curious, scrabbling movement. The man hardly touched Sammy. Everyone would swear to that—just the faintest brushing of his hand against the dirty white shoulder, a reflexive gesture of disgust and confusion. But Sammy wasn't taking no for an answer. He made the most of that slight push. There was the fluid grace of his body flying through the air.

"*Oooo-oooohhhh!*" A sigh of relief magnified to agony.

"No, no . . . Oh, yes, *yes!*" Angelo yelled. But the sound of his voice stopped, as the ringing of a small bell is stopped by the sudden enclosure of a hand.

Everything was silent. A group of nurses' aides in gray uniforms crowded into the doorway behind the priest and the nuns. The man and the two women in black stared down at Sammy without comprehension. The skinny old woman from the hospital coffee shop held her hand up over her mouth; the custodians gaped like frogs. It was such a clear, wonderful day.

And Sammy lay arched over the wrought-iron rail at the foot of the steps, looking grotesquely comfortable. He was impaled on the decorative spike; a small bit of the iron showed an even fresher coating of color between the buttons of his shirt.

Angelo looked around jerkily, filled with a fevered curiosity: he didn't want to miss anything. Yes, all the people did look shocked; perhaps stunned and sickened. Yet no one was foolish enough for pity. Angelo felt that it was somehow up to him. He searched for response like a man with no nerve endings whose clothes were on fire. He looked at the surrounding faces. He looked at the sky. He looked at Sammy, and a use-worn part of him wanted to lift the figure from the spike, to do what was reasonable: bind arteries, stitch up puncture wounds, repair lacerations. But something more profound held him back. He wanted Sammy to stay there, to stay and suffer that immolation over and over and over.

Oh, yeah, Sammy, I get it, I get it.

And Angelo began to laugh. Great gobbets of mirth came up in his throat, each succeeded by a larger one. The two women in black dresses shrank behind the frightened man, and all the spectators looked at him with a horror far more intense than any emotion Sammy had aroused.

Oh, I get it!

He laughed harder and harder, and people began to move. The priest stepped forward; an interne walked cautiously out of the doorway and headed for Sammy. Time was no object. Angelo began to strangle as Sammy tried to laugh with him, and the sweat was wrung out of him like thin, dark oil on his skin. He was convulsed. Tears streamed down his face.

Sister Louise stepped out quickly, unaware that anything had happened. And then she saw, and was instantly destroyed in a way that would insist upon her living.

Angelo was bent in two; the laughter would not stop. He slipped to the ground and drew his knees up to his chest; the pain was unbelievable, but the laughter went on. Through his tears he seemed to see Sammy's eyes become lusterless. Other voices tried to drown him out, but they didn't have a chance. How it hurt now—straight up through his guts to his heart.

He was moved by people's hands, rolled over, and still the laughter went on wrenching him apart. He was blinded, maddened, devastated by it, but it was his, and he gripped it like the last branch on earth. And then it spurted out of him and was gone, and he fell back limply, staring up at the sky.

Everything was so blue and white.

And then nothing.

CHAPTER SEVENTEEN

CEILINGS, he thought, remembering how patients on stretchers had looked. He studied the open cracks of his bedroom ceiling, and the cracks that had been crudely healed by plaster, and it seemed he began to understand why the patients stared upward so fixedly. He recalled Maria Alvarez —it was on the day he had first seen Sammy—and how she had watched the ceilings change as they wheeled her onto the elevator and then off again onto another floor. A ceiling permitted contemplation; for all its complexity, it never doubled back on you.

I wanted him there.

He followed great Amazonian cracks, veered off with them

into deeper, thinner offshoots, tacked off those to follow pale, nervous tributaries, which in turn flowered off into rivulets so fine that they were lost in the dusk of late day.

I wanted him there.

For weeks he lay on his bed, watching that inverted terrain change with the weather or the hour. He woke early when the vast plain was a soft, pearly gray. Gradually, he would notice blue in the gray, then violet, then a soft rose. Rose warmed to peach, and so to orange, and sound would seem to come from the ceiling instead of from the house and the street.

Dominic and Esther were awed and frightened by his illness because they could not understand it, any more than the doctor, who told them Angelo had had a mild nervous collapse and that several weeks of rest and quiet, along with the prescribed medication, would repair him.

The first few days after he had been brought home like a drunk they had tried to talk to him, to entice speech from him by offering things he should have needed; it was as though they hoped to expose sham. But he had asked for nothing and would not answer. After that, Esther would put his food on the little table between the two beds, next to the medicines the doctor had left. He would eat normally after she left the room, and when it was necessary, he got up to go to the bathroom. But he looked at nothing on the way; his vision was reserved for the ceiling.

Sometimes he was aware that their voices were being subdued for his sake. More often he would hear Theresa's slippered feet come into his room, and feel the bed sag as she sat beside him. Distantly, he would notice that she was getting frailer and more ugly, with an ugliness that somehow defined her; where there had been only blandness, where her face had been a smooth and completely opaque covering, there was now a tangle of moving and tormented features. Her face became, unbearably, a human face, and her breath smelled bad. And with her beside him, he would feel a cold trickle of pain.

When Dominic woke in the morning, he looked across the room, and always experienced the same inchoate feeling that something immense seethed in his nephew's head. Angelo's dark hair was overgrown so it dwarfed his face; his black thin beard made him look like some desert dweller dying of thirst just short of a well. He seemed to have no need to blink or move, and Dominic wondered if he ever slept.

The air turned cooler as September passed its mid-point. They closed the window except for a few inches on top, and that lowering of the window frame cast a dimness over part of the ceiling, a shadow that moved with the changing light and that had no place there.

Angelo looked at the four walls, at the doorway, at the window, at the books on his dresser, imagining deliverance, pretending that he had in truth been left unharmed. He wedged the pillow up under his neck and began for the first time in many weeks to think rationally about what had happened. A creature had been extinguished and had become rubbish; there was an explanation for it, but no reason. So to all intents and purposes he *was* well again, and he abandoned the ceiling and slept, exhausted, all that day and through the night.

The next morning when Dominic woke, he saw the change. Angelo lay sleeping on his side, hugging the pillow. His dark young beard was like a fungus on his smooth, olive skin, and for some odd reason his broken nose only made him look younger. Something about him moved Dominic; he felt a sadness for himself and for his nephew, but there was nothing he could do about it.

Later that morning, Angelo got up very carefully and went into the bathroom, feeling some pride in the way he was able to handle himself so that he felt no pain, and took a bath. His body seemed strange and soft to him in the tub; later, when he shaved, he avoided his own eyes. Take it slow and easy at first, he told himself. You'll be as good as ever, soon.

He dressed and walked out past Esther, who clapped a hand over her mouth, and sat on the porch steps in the sunshine. The trees were faintly touched with color and the air smelled of leaves. He felt a trickle of enjoyment in just the sight of the street. There was the bunting over the wires, most of it looking quite old now. Across the street, the Madonna's little moat was almost choked with reddish leaves. The bald grocer stepped outside furtively, glanced toward Angelo, and slowly backed into his store again. Angelo leaned his head back against the warm wood of the house, and smiled slightly.

I was sick and now I'm well. He looked at chlorophyll green, oxygen blue. The sun blinked on the mirror-encrusted peacock and he grinned at it; he knew the speed of light.

Confidently, he said, "Sammy," and it did nothing to him. The heat felt good on his face.

When he got hungry he went inside and asked his mother for something to eat. She gazed at him, her desire to love him so strong that it nearly became love.

"It was almost a month," she said. "I can't tell you what it did to me."

"I'm okay now," he said. "You don't have to worry."

"No, no . . ." Her voice showed that she remembered what was and what never could be between them; his getting up out of bed was not a metamorphosis, merely a thaw.

He ate with Theresa standing next to his chair, and when

178

he went back outside, she followed him and sat on the steps beside him. He noticed that her skin had a blue cast and that she breathed with odd, short gasps. She's sick, he thought. But he would not tamper with her; he would just follow the same old pattern.

"See how the leaves are changing, Theresa," he said in his special voice. "Them are *deciduous* trees, that's why they do that. It'll get colder. Then one morning there'll be ice on the grass. You like to make marks on the window when there's frost, don't you? I tell you, I couldn't of taken another hot day myself. The winter's better for me. The air is clearer."

Some of the neighborhood people passed, glancing toward the brother and sister curiously. One or two nodded. The shadows became longer.

A man came down the street carrying a shapeless briefcase, looking slightly incongruous in a summer straw hat with a bright, paisley band. He stopped in front of Angelo, who recognized him as the seedy insurance man who had collected on a twenty-five-cent-a-week policy from Esther for years and years.

"Whatta ya say, DeMarco," he said. "You remember me, Dorfman?"

Angelo nodded.

"I got a little business here for you. Could we go inside?"

"Me?"

"Nobody else," Dorfman said with the sumptuous smile of someone who knows he can please you at no cost to himself.

They went into the living room. Esther heard them and came from the kitchen, her face irritated and slightly worried.

"You want me, Dorfman?" she said.

"No, not this time, Mrs. DeMarco. This time I deal with

your sonny boy." What began as joviality shifted over into gravity as Dorfman recalled the nature of his business.

Angelo stared at him in bewilderment.

"As you know, my company is connected nationally," Dorfman said with pride. In reality it was a second-rate firm that had often been in trouble. "We got agents in all parts, and our policies are transferred from here to there daily."

"What is it, Dorfman?" Esther demanded.

Dorfman looked piqued. "I'll get to the point," he said. He opened his briefcase, which was filled with paper, and pulled out a long, green-decorated folder. "It appears I got a little death payment."

"What death payment?" Esther asked. "Nobody died."

"Not for *you*," Dorfman said smugly. "For *him*." He pointed at Angelo. "He's a beneficiary."

"Whatta you talking about?" Angelo demanded.

"If you will both be patient, I will explain," Dorfman answered. "It seems that we of Utah National have had a funny policy for years and years with a certain man. Actually, we have lost considerable money on the bookkeeping alone, which has added up to more than our commission, because this man, now deceased, has changed his beneficiary almost two dozen times. Practically twice a year he changed to someone else on this big-deal five-hundred-dollar policy. Well, DeMarco, you're the winner, the last one."

"Who are you talking about?" Angelo asked with his eyes closed.

"One Samuel Abel Kahan, lately an employee of Sacred Heart Hospital."

Angelo swallowed carefully, his eyes still closed, his body motionless. Esther didn't understand.

"It's double indemnity, too, for accidental death," Dorfman said almost gaily, as though he were profiting.

"Who is it?" Esther asked.

"That orderly that died in that funny accident. It was in the papers, a whole crazy deal with that rape case, and then it came out that this guy was stealing drugs or something."

"Oh." Esther remembered its connection with Angelo's illness. "Oh, that," she said.

Angelo still sat with his eyes closed, his body frozen in the afternoon light.

Dorfman cleared his throat and tried one of his professional lines. "I know these things can be delicate. One feels guilty about profiting from a loved one's death. But then . . ."

Angelo began shaking his head, so Dorfman took another tried-and-true course.

"One can naturally understand how moving it is when we are presented with the evidence of our loved one's foresight and . . ."

Angelo continued shaking his head, but now a convulsive movement swept his body, and it was apparent that he was about to laugh. His mouth bent as the thing moved up through his body. The insurance man nodded approvingly; Esther smiled.

And then Angelo began to weep.

The insurance man licked his lips. Esther dropped her smile in alarm. The sobbing filled the room, and Angelo bit on his knuckles to choke the ugly sound.

"Now, now, sonny, I know how these things are," the insurance man said; he had seen it all before.

"Shut up," Angelo snarled. He wiped his eyes and stood, the shell of a street fighter now, but still possessed of his own decorum. "You don't know why I'm crying, any more than *I* do."

In bitter silence the brief business was consummated, and the insurance man left the house.

Angelo took the check and lay down on the couch to study it. After she had watched him for a while, from the doorway, Esther went into the kitchen, treading softly, as she had during the weeks of his illness. From time to time she came timidly to look at him, holding the pale blue slip of paper in his hand. It seemed that he counted the sum by ones, over and over, and the peculiar intensity of his study made her wonder if he was going to be sick again.

The day declined and left him in shadow, so that he could not read; but by then he had reproduced the check in his brain.

"What're you going to do with it?" Esther asked in the early dark. "It's a good piece of money, a thousand dollars."

Angelo looked at her sturdy figure in the doorway; she seemed a long distance away from him. Perhaps it was just that sense of unbridgeable distance that made him feel a touch of tenderness. Theresa came up behind her and peered over her shoulder into the darkness where he lay, and the two of them were like a picture in an old album; they moved him because he could bear to be moved, because they were so far away.

"I mean it's yours, of course, no one's going to try and chisel any of it," Esther said, pressing for an answer.

"I don't know yet, I'm not sure what I'll do."

There was nothing for Esther to even sigh about. She left Theresa alone in the doorway, watching him, and went to her kitchen, where she was more sure of herself.

Angelo helped Frank in the store throughout the winter; a young Greek kid took care of the hospital deliveries. Theresa got very sick. The doctor said she had a congenital heart ailment. What it meant was that she died in February, in her own bed and in her own night.

Esther did all the crying and Dominic hid most of the time. Angelo did neither; he had laughed his agony and cried his relief, and all his sister's death was to him was an enlargement of Sammy's death. He moved and spoke gracefully and quietly, and no one knew that he did so as a precaution. Frank said to Dominic one day, "Theresa dying changed him, Dom. You can see it made him gentler." How could they know that Theresa's death was only part of the one death, and that it had not made him gentle, but only cautious and quiet; he never again wanted to miss hearing what happened in silence.

In April, with nothing to keep him there, he gave Esther half the insurance money and left home; he had the dim, shy hope that some other place might be better for him.

He went away in sunlight. The trees were new again. The shrewish Madonna looked disconsolately at her choked lily pond; someone had thrown in some orange rinds, too. But the dazzling peacock lorded it over the entire street.

The kind of person he still was, he wouldn't have walked ten feet out of his way in memory of anything; he still did not believe in death, was still convinced it deserved no more than a period. But the hospital was on his way to the bus station. The day was as bright and clear as the day on which Samuel Abel Kahan had died. Shadows were richly black and etched out each brick in the hospital wall. A few of the windows on the far wing of the old building were already X'ed for destruction. McKenna stopped in a doorway to wave at him; Angelo waved back. A black figure in a window might or might not have been Sister Louise; he didn't look to see.

As he passed the new building, his arm felt tired; the suitcase was heavy with books, and he set it down. The lower floors were finally glassed in, but those near the top were still open to the air. As he looked up at the high whiteness, a bird darted out of a dark rectangle and flew upward in ascending spirals against the flame-blue sky. He shaded his eyes to follow its flight.

"Just another goddam pigeon," he said.

He picked up his suitcase and took a last look around. Nothing altered the clarity of the sunlight.

He began to walk toward the bus station.

Suddenly he seemed to hear the dim burble of children's laughter coming from the pavilion, behind the main building where he couldn't see it, and in that distant, cascading sound, carried like a chip on a torrent, he thought he heard the word *boychik*. And a blade twitched into his heart, beginning that slow, massive bleeding he would never be able to stop, no matter what else he might accomplish. He was surprised and puzzled as he walked with that mortal wound in him, for it occurred to him that, although the wound would be the death of him, it would be the life of him too.